VALLEY OF VICE

by

Steve Garcia

Dales Large Print Books
Long Preston, North Yorkshire,
BD23 4ND, England.

British Library Cataloguing in Publication Data.

Garcia, Steve
    Valley of vice.

    A catalogue record of this book is
    available from the British Library

    ISBN   978-1-84262-766-2 pbk

Dales Large Print is an imprint of Library Magna Books Ltd.

Printed and bound in Great Britain by
T.J. (International) Ltd., Cornwall, PL28 8RW

Prologue

Three months earlier

'A snafu, Duke. That's what it is, and it's up to you to un-fuck it.' Simons rapped his gold Cross pen on the edge of the desk. There were already ten years' of tiny dents in the desk molding from his nervous tapping and he added a few more. The numbers on the digital desk clock glowed bright red – 12.10. Muriel wasn't scheduled to be back from lunch for about twenty minutes but Simons couldn't take the chance of her overhearing the conversation. He got up and crossed the room, the ten-foot phone cord stretched behind him like a tether. He glanced out, saw no one, and closed the office door. He couldn't trust Muriel to take a full lunch hour. She was too dedicated and too honest. 'We need to move fast. Pearl is a Section Eight. He's going to come undone being locked up.'

'He's not a Rock of Gibraltar like you, Councilman?'

Simons bit his lip. He flinched and let out a small groan. 'The fucker is crazy. You have to make sure he doesn't talk.'

'Hey, dumbass, try to follow along. They nailed Pearl for shooting a cop. I can't waltz in there like he got a speeding ticket and fix it.'

'I understand. But if he has kept his trap shut, so far at least, maybe you can make sure he keeps it shut. Can't you smuggle something in to keep him happy?'

'Maybe. I need to let things cool off a bit before I go poking around in there.'

'He'll squeal.'

'No, he won't. I may not be able to get to him this minute, but he knows if he flips on me that there would be no place on this good earth for him to hide.'

'Listen to me. Pearl is a whacked-out junkie. Unstable. When the need for a fix overwhelms him, he won't be thinking straight. If it gets too hot in there, and it will, he'll give us up for a cinnamon Tic Tac. We need to make sure that doesn't happen.'

'Are you telling me how to do my job?'

'I'm not telling you *how* to do it, I'm simply telling you to do it now.'

'You should know that I don't take well to being threatened, Theo.'

'No threat.' Simons grabbed his can of cold Mountain Dew and took a gulp. He had seen Duke's work in Iraq and didn't want to get into a pissing match with a cold-blooded psycho. The silence on the other end of the line stretched Simons' nerves.

Obviously the pills the doctor prescribed for his anxiety weren't worth a damn. 'Duke? Come on. Say something. We can meet if you want and figure out a plan.'

'I don't think so.'

'All right then. Do something.'

'Or else?'

'Goddamn it. Quit looking to pick a fight with me. Our problem is sitting down at the Central Jail.'

Silence filled the phone line again. Simons took his Fresh Air Ashtray out of the top drawer and clicked it on. The small motor whirred. He reached into his jacket pocket, pulled out a pack of Kools and lit up. The smoke he exhaled was sucked in by the tiny whirring fans.

'You're a bastard.' Simons' breathing was labored. 'Iraq is in the past.'

'You're the one who can't get over it. I think I'm more worried about you cracking than Pearl. Take your pills or talk to your shrink or whatever it is you do to keep a grip on reality. Meanwhile, I'll see if I can find out something about our boy.'

Simons' hand shook slightly as he took a deep drag on the cigarette. 'That's what I'm talking about – team work. I have your back, you have mine. Right?'

A dial tone was the only response Simons got. He put the phone in its cradle, leaned back in his black leather chair and crossed his arms. He rocked forward and back as his eyes wandered around the room, finally settling on a five by seven photograph of his wife and children.

God, don't let this blow up in my face. It would kill Teri and the kids. And my folks. They won't know what to do – what to say.

Simons unlocked the second drawer of his desk and pulled it open. Inside was a wooden box made from polished cedar which he took out and placed on the desk. He read the dedication inscribed on the small metal plate affixed to the top. *Captain Theodore Simons. A Troop, 1st Squadron, 4th US. Cavalry, DOU6, Desert Storm.* Inside, nestled in red velvet, was an ivory handled Colt .45 Peacemaker revolver. It had been a gift from his men when the unit came home. He could still remember Duke's stinging words when he delivered it to the hospital. 'It's like General Patton's. Everything considered, I should slap the shit out of you instead of giving you the gun.'

Simons laid his cigarette in the ashtray and took a bottle of Vat 69 Scotch whiskey and a small glass from his drawer. He blew into the glass to remove any dust, a habit he had since his desert days, and poured a shot. In an unbroken motion, he downed the amber liquid, slammed the glass on his desk and poured another.

He removed the gun from the box. Slowly turning it in his hands, he admired the weapon and was proud of the fact that his men thought so highly of him – except Duke, of course.

He took a final drag on the cigarette and dropped it into the nearly empty can of soda.

With a lint-free rag he wiped the gun. He sighted down the barrel, aiming at a photograph of his old army unit that hung on the far wall.

'Bang,' he said quietly. Then he spun the chamber to make sure the gun was loaded.

1

Salvador Reyes had spent the last two hours shuffling papers, eating almonds and watching the clock. Quiet days at the Hollywood Precinct were also boring days. Unfortunately, he and Phil had to pull the extra duty today and the OT pay didn't seem worth it.

Ray Brooks entered the detective's cubicle area. 'How's life in the Pit?'

He received a couple of grunts.

'So, is everybody going to Jerry Cresner's welcome back party at the Wilcox? It starts at eight o'clock which, by my watch, is right about now.'

'Kahn and I are,' Wagner said. 'Willy T. makes some of the best Buffalo wings in the city. That alone is a good enough reason to go.'

'I'm in. How about you, Joanne?' Albanese said. 'I'll buy you a drink.'

Joanne Coombs nodded. 'I don't know Cresner, but a drink sounds good.'

Reyes laughed. 'So basically, except for our good sergeant, you're all going for the food and drinks.'

'The reason doesn't matter,' Brooks said. 'We need a crowd there to make him feel good. He was my partner back in the day. I transferred over here – oh hell – a long time ago now. Jerry stayed in Robbery.'

'He's been on medical leave, right?' Coombs asked.

'Yeah. He was busting up a mugging. The mugger shot him in the hip, severed some artery in his pelvis. First of all, they didn't know if he'd make it. Then they said he probably wouldn't walk again. But here it is, three months later and he's returning to limited duty.'

Reyes and his partner, Philippa Wallace, watched the others leave.

'Want to take an early dinner?' she said. 'We could grab a sandwich at the Wilcox. That way we could be there for at least part of Cresner's party.'

'Anything is better than sitting here.'

Reyes and Wallace moved their car from the rear parking lot of the station to a spot a few feet down from the front door of the Wilcox 'just in case'. As they entered the bar they were immediately greeted by the owner, Willy Truss.

'Hey. Hello, hello. Two of my favorite people. Check out my sign.' He pointed at a sign hanging on the back wall. *Welcome Back Jerry.*

Reyes gave him a thumbs-up. 'Nice, Willy. You the man.'

'Ain't nobody else,' he said. 'Hey Phil, how long is a good-looking sister like you going to hang with that *chulo?*'

'He's my daytime boy-toy,' Wallace said.

'Hey now,' Reyes said. They all laughed.

Reyes and Wallace looked around for the others from their squad. 'Boy-toy?' Reyes said.

She smiled. 'Willy is a nice old guy. He likes it when women flirt with him.'

The Wilcox Avenue Canteen was down the street from the station. It had been there since before Prohibition and had long been considered a cops' bar. The walls were filled with pictures of officers and criminals. Framed newspaper front pages of famous cases surrounded a small glass case where novels about the LAPD were on display. On a polished wood plaque were one by three-inch brass plates inscribed with the names of officers who had fallen in the line of duty. Next to it was another similar plaque but

11

the list was of officers who had been patrons of the bar and had retired from the force. The third and fourth plaques contained the names of officers who had been on, or currently were on, The Wilcox Avenue Canteen Bowling Team.

Wallace and Reyes made their way through the groups of officers from all across LA to a table where Coombs and Albanese sat. Reyes could hear snippets of conversations as he passed by.

'It's too soon. He was still in a wheelchair a few days ago.'

'I wouldn't be surprised if he doesn't show.'

'You never know what a bullet can do to your insides – or to your psyche.'

'Have a seat,' Albanese said.

'Where are the rest of the guys?' He pushed a plate of bones toward the center of the table.

'That's Wagner's. He scarfed those down, then he and Kahn went to shoot some pool. Is Wagner any good? He made it sound like he was a hustler.'

'He thinks he's a lot of things,' Reyes said.

More officers wandered in; the noise in the room increased. 'There's my old buddy, Olivia Hughes,' Wallace said. 'I'm going to go say hi to her. I'll be back in a few minutes.'

'I'm going get something to drink,' Reyes said. 'Anybody else need anything?'

'I'll pass,' Coombs said. She lifted her

glass slightly. 'Still nursing this one.'

Albanese shook his head. 'No thanks.'

Reyes scooted his chair back and walked to the bar. 'Hey Willy, can I have a Coke?'

'Sure thing.' He turned to grab a glass and Reyes noticed the slight limp from his prosthetic leg. Willy had stepped in the wrong spot while on patrol in Vietnam and a mine took his left leg below the knee. He always joked that he'd been drafted and shipped to Vietnam as a nigger and came back labeled a baby-killer. That should have been enough to piss off any man. But Willy was somehow above all of that stuff. He went right to work as a bartender and eventually bought into the Wilcox when one of the partners decided to retire. Willy's first official act as a co-owner was to put up a sign that read: *Stop The Hate.* It still hung behind the bar. A few days later he put up a POW-MIA sign. That was still there, too.

'Here ya go my friend, one ice cold Coca-Cola.'

'Jesus H. Cheesecake,' Joe Donawald said as he sidled up to Reyes and slapped him on the back. 'Coke? You on the wagon, Sal?'

'Hi Joe. No, still on duty though.'

'Ah. You had me worried there for a minute. How's your boy?'

'Nando is great, thanks. Still in the clutches of his mother and grandfather but there's nothing I can do about that.'

'Good luck with that mess. Say, I'm looking for someone to shoot pool with. Wagner and Kahn are back there taking on all corners. Want to help me whip their asses?'

'Nah. Not today.'

'No? Do you know anybody that can play?'

'Albanese shoots a pretty mean stick. Come on, he's sitting with me.' They walked over to the table. 'You guys know Joe Donawald?'

'Sure, I've seen you guys around,' Donawald nodded.

'Joe wants to take on our pool hustlers. You interested Emilio?'

Albanese grinned. 'Why not?' He stood up but Donawald held him in place. 'Do you guys know how you can tell if you're in a lesbian bar?' No one answered. 'Even the pool table doesn't have balls.'

'I hope you shoot pool better than you tell jokes,' said Albanese. The two made their way across the room, squeezing between small groups of cops. Every stool at the bar as well as every table and booth were now occupied. People stood wherever they could find space.

Coombs and Reyes suddenly found themselves alone at the table. 'I've signed up for a night class in Spanish offered by UCLA Continuing Ed,' she said. 'Are you still willing to tutor me?'

'You know I will.'

'How about tonight? My class starts next week. I haven't looked at a Spanish textbook since high school.'

'I should be free. You doing it for the incentive pay or so you can be a translator?'

'A little of both I guess.'

'Did you know that if I wanted to be an interpreter, I have to take the class first?'

'It does seem odd that a native Mexican needs a class,' she said, 'but it's not only about the translating. It's about proper procedure when dealing with a non-English speaking Latino.'

'It's still bullshit.' Reyes took a drink of his Coke. 'Did I tell you my ex is marrying the son of a bitch she was seeing behind my back? One of her daddy's corporate toadies – David Nowitzski.'

'Yeah, you mentioned it. That sucks, Sal.'

'I know what you're going to say – that I need to move on. It'd probably be easier if Nando wasn't living with them.' Even as he was spouting off, Reyes wished he had kept his mouth shut. It seemed that every time he and Joanne had five minutes together, his ex-wife' s life somehow managed to work its way into the conversation, blowing out any spark like an ill wind.

'Can I join you?' Without waiting for a response, Captain Siley took the seat that Albanese had vacated. 'What's everybody drinking?' He threw a twenty-dollar bill on the table. 'Next round is on me.'

'I'm persuaded,' Coombs said. 'What are

you having, Captain?'

'I'll take a rum and Coke with lime.' He looked around the room full of police. 'Where's Cresner?'

'Haven't seen him,' Reyes said.

Coombs took the twenty and excused herself. 'Did anyone check on him to make sure that he was okay?'

'I didn't, but then I don't really know him.'

'That stupid ass shouldn't be coming back on duty yet. Where's Brooks? Brooks should call him. They're old friends.'

'I know he's here. Why don't I go see if I can find him?' Reyes stood and passed Coombs at the bar. She was in her civvies now, and looked damn good. 'I'll be right back,' he said to her. 'I'm going to find Brooks and have him call our missing guest of honor.'

Coombs frowned. Reyes knew what that look meant. She wasn't happy, but when it came to being the one who got stuck with Captain 'Dry' Siley, it was everyone for themselves. Siley was a bit of a pain, but worse than that, he was boring – dust in the mouth boring.

Reyes crossed the room, high-fived a couple of officers and stopped to talk for a few seconds with Kahn, who was enjoying Wilcox's signature Double Pepper Jack Cheeseburger with creamy jalapeno sauce and caramelized onions.

'I thought you were shooting pool.'

'Wagner needed a break.' Kahn held up the greasy burger as though it were the Holy Grail. 'I'm going to enjoy eating this. Angie and her scented aromatherapy candles don't stand a chance. Tonight, if only for an hour or so, I will be king of my apartment once again.'

'The only thing your ass will rule tonight is the couch.' Reyes stepped around Kahn and walked into the men's room. *Less than an hour and Joanne and I will be practicing a little Spanish and maybe, if I get lucky...*

Wagner was at the urinal and was mumbling out loud. Reyes hesitated. Wagner was breaking all the rules of etiquette in a men's room – taking the middle urinal, talking, looking around and, if Reyes stepped up, Wagner would engage him in a conversation, sure as shit.

Wagner turned slightly. 'Come on. There's always room for one more.'

Reyes stepped up and zipped down. He stared straight ahead but Wagner became animated and started bitching about Albanese being a hustler.

'Damn Wops. You can't trust them.'

'Uh-huh,' Reyes said.

'So who is that blond bitch hanging with Blaylock? Ya know her?'

'Blond bitch? You mean Tripucka?'

'Could be. She's hot. I think I'm going to

go for some of that.'

They finished at almost the same moment. 'Better proceed with caution. Beer and blondes with badges don't mix. At least not for you.'

'Oh man. You hurt my feelings. Have I ever offended a fellow officer?'

'You're kidding, right? I'm telling you, if they put your brain in a pickle jar in some side show at the circus, I'd pay to see it.'

'I got your pickle right here,' Wagner said as he grabbed his crotch.

Wallace pushed open the men's room door. 'Hey Sal, let's go. We've got a call.'

'Okay, I'm coming.'

'Hey!' Wagner yelled as the door closed. 'You didn't wash your hands.'

Wallace was moving through the bar and heading for the exit. 'What do we have?' Reyes asked.

'There's been a fire at an indie studio a few blocks from Paramount. Melrose and St. Andrew's. Some place called Green Cheese Entertainment. They've found a body in the debris.'

'Accident or arson?'

'Nothing yet, but they want a whole team there and we get to be the detectives.'

'Oh, goody.' Reyes checked the clock on the wall as he hustled through the crowd to Coombs. 20.20. *Hardly worth coming.* Siley was standing and speaking with someone

18

else. Reyes leaned on the table and looked at Coombs. *'Me tengo que ir,'* he said. 'That means, "I have to go".'

'What's up?'

'We've got a possible arson, with at least one fatality.'

'Hmm. I hope this isn't an excuse to get out of helping me with Spanish.'

'I'll call you if it turns out to be nothing.' Reyes hurried toward the door. He waved at Willy T. 'Save me some wings.'

'I'll put some fresh ones on the fire,' the barman replied.

2

'Damn,' Wallace said. 'Look at all the gawkers.' She parked the car down the street, out of the way of the fire engines and grabbed the radio. 'This is Adam Six Nineteen. We're Code Six at the Green Cheese fire.'

'Roger Adam Six Nineteen.'

'I guess we should be grateful the fire wasn't at one of the big studios. We'd be there for a month trying to get through the crowd.' They got out of the car and made their way toward the scene. The air was heavy with smoke and filled with the clanking and whirring noises from the fire trucks and the steady hiss of water being sprayed on the last areas of the blaze. Wallace paused and checked what remained of the structure. Steel beams jutted like broken ribs through the charred carcass. The roof had apparently collapsed into the building, blowing out portions of the side walls. There was a peculiar aluminum-looking crane-like arm poking up higher than everything else. *Not part of the building. Something they had brought in?* At some point, maybe when the windows shattered or the roof came down, some of the building's contents were scattered into the street. Most of it was typical stuff – papers, broken furniture and such, but this fire had something a little different in the debris field. Costumes. There were hats, dresses, wigs and God knows what else. It made it appear as though dozens of people had simply been vaporized.

'Have it figured out yet?' Reyes asked.

'I'm going to go with a fire.'

'Good one. How do you do it?'

'Years of practice.'

The detectives eased their way through the people who had gathered to watch the fire. When they reached the barricades, Wallace greeted the uniform on crowd control. 'Hi, Forston.'

'Hi. So you guys get this one, huh? Good luck. Barclay-Jones is over with the others.'

'The assistant DA?' Reyes asked. 'Why

would the DA's office send someone to a fire, even if it is arson?'

'Election time,' Forston said. 'Fires bring out the media. Free coverage.'

Reyes looked around. 'There's no TV here.'

'Come and gone. They stayed long enough to get the good stuff, then beat it back to make the evening news.'

'Who are the first responders?' Wallace asked.

'These guys.' Forston gestured toward the onlookers. 'Like the proverbial moths to a flame, huh? Geez, does a fire ever draw them out of the woodwork.' He turned and scanned the scene. 'You want Hastings and Marcell. There's Hastings.' He pointed to a small group gathered near a fire truck. 'I think you guys are the last two members of the team to arrive.'

'We like to be fashionably late,' Wallace said. She and Reyes took a few steps toward the distant fire truck and stopped. 'Hold it a minute.' Wallace stared at the smoldering rubble that had been, a few hours earlier, the home of Green Cheese Entertainment. 'There's not much left of the place but smoke.' She pointed at a set of spotlights at the back of the scene. 'CSI must be here.'

They stepped over puddles, hoses, chunks of rubble and a wig or two as they made their way past the firefighters who continued to pour water on to a couple of

21

hotspots. Reyes tapped one firefighter on the back. 'Can't get it out?'

'Little pockets of fire under the collapsed walls and debris piles. Hard to get water in there,' the firefighter said. 'We're going to go in and move that shit around. It won't be long and we'll be done. Then you can start.'

'Not exactly what I had planned for tonight.'

'Tell me about it. I was cooking up my mother's chili for the firehouse.'

'You should have brought it along and cooked it on the fire.'

'Wouldn't have worked. It's a Five Alarm chili so it's even hotter than this.'

Reyes chuckled. 'I'll have to try it sometime.'

Wallace eyed the investigation team as she approached. Marcell was okay. Hastings seemed a bit weird at times. He named his shotgun 'tulip', but his performance was always top notch. Assistant DA Barclay-Jones. Strait-laced professional. Sometimes rode cops a bit hard. Ed Withingham from Crime Scene Investigation. Nerdy kind of guy, okay to work with. A bit slow but that was because he was methodical and careful. Lewis Drake the photographer. All in all, not a bad group.

'Hi,' Wallace said. 'You all know my partner, Sal Reyes?'

'I don't think I do,' Barclay-Jones said. She

shook hands with Reyes who smiled and nodded. The others nodded or muttered greetings.

Wallace looked around. 'Where's the ME?'

'Doctor Hackett's at the back of the structure. By our spotlights.' Withingham gestured toward the glare. 'We didn't find the body until a short while ago, so he hasn't had a lot of time to look things over.' Withingham looked down at the small burn on the side of his left shoe. 'Look at that. A brand new pair, ruined.'

'Too bad,' Wallace said. 'I guess that's part of the cost of doing business. So, who found the body?'

'We did. My team,' Withingham said. 'The entire back corner of the building collapsed. We were raking the debris. When we pulled down a stack about a yard high, we discovered a metal desk and a metal cabinet that had fallen over. There was a body partially concealed under all of that.'

'Were you able to determine anything from your initial exam?'

'I'm afraid not.' Withingham adjusted his dark-rimmed glasses and stared at his notepad. 'The body was pretty badly charred. Before we dug around too much we figured we should get Doctor Hackett over here. While we were waiting on him, I was able to determine that victim was a male. Under six foot tall. My assistants are back there giving

Doctor Hackett a hand.'

'I guess we should head back there then and see what the Doc has found,' Wallace said. 'Hastings. Got anything to add?'

'Not much,' Hastings said. 'When we got here the building was fully engaged. We checked to see if entering the building was possible or even a good idea. There was no way. I mean, smoke was belching from every window and we could hear that groaning sound that you hear right before the whole mess comes down. We decided the best thing – hell, the only thing – we could do was get the people in the street back and out of the way. That's what we did. Then let's see, the fire department arrived. A short while later, the roof caved in. I think that's about, right, Marcell?'

'We did check with the gathered masses,' Marcell said. 'Nothing much. They said there's been a lot of construction work going on. An old hotel on the lot next to Green Cheese was torn down for a new building, but mostly there's been a lot of renovation. It's driving some of the homeless from their cubby holes in some of these buildings. We were thinking maybe one of the displaced homeless guys accidentally set it on fire or, a second guess, one of the construction workers left a torch on.'

'I hope you're right,' Wallace said. The last thing she needed for her quarterly stats was another unsolved homicide. 'Has the owner of the building been contacted?'

'Yup,' Hastings said. 'His name is Johnny Jin Moon and he said he was on his way.'

'Anything else?' Wallace looked back toward the bright lights and spotted the shadowy figure of Dr. Hackett. She had worked for him a long time ago. He was thorough, but wasted no time. Get in, do your job, get the hell out of the way. That's what he used to tell her. It was a good policy.

'Not really,' Marcell said. 'The rest of the gawkers offered nothing. They saw nothing. They didn't know if anyone was inside. Typical stuff.'

'Thanks. Mr Withingham,' Wallace said. 'What are your thoughts about the fire's origin?'

'If you ask me to make a guess, I suspect the fire started across the way from the room where we found the body. I can't prove it yet. That's simply experience talking. There was flammable stuff all over the place. We won't know until we can rake the coals back.'

'Thanks everybody. We're going to head back and see Doctor Hackett.' Wallace and Reyes started walking along the street. A few of the fire crews were beginning to clean up, pack their equipment and take a breather. One hose crew continued to pour water on a steaming pile of wreckage. Most of the on-lookers were gone, some likely hurrying to a computer to upload their pictures to CNN for an iReport.

'You know Sal, I think Marcell was right.' Her eyes continued to take in the scene as they walked. 'They're going to find that the guy was homeless and broke into the building for a nap and accidentally set the fire. There's usually a boat-load of accelerants at construction sites. The bum flips his cigarette into some plastic drop cloth. It catches fire and wham, bam, it ignites the turpentine and bye-bye building, bye-bye bum.'

As they rounded the corner Reyes pointed toward the ruins, where a jutting piece of metal was poking up like the arm of a fallen robot. 'What in the hell do you think that crane-like thing is? It's got to be twenty feet long...'

'I don't know. It is a movie studio. Maybe it's a prop.' She stopped in front of a chain link fence. Small signs wired to the fence read *MAC Construction. Keep Out.*

'We can cut through here,' Reyes said. 'Ready to climb?'

'Climb? Isn't there an easier way? How the hell did old Doctor Hackett get back there with all those lights? They didn't crawl over this damn fence, did they?'

Reyes was already over. 'Come on. It's shorter this way.'

'Shorter than what?' Wallace asked as she climbed the shaky chain link fence. 'Sal.

26

Shorter than what?' She jumped down and landed on a rock, slightly twisting her right ankle and stumbled forward. *Not again.* It was getting to be her Achilles heel. 'Damn it. I'm too old to be hopping over fences. This better be necessary.'

'Well, it does look like there might be a back way in,' Reyes said. 'Probably for deliveries, but we'd have to go all the way around the block. This is shorter and faster.'

Wallace muttered as they crossed the lot. Water from fighting the fire had spilled into the site and now it was not only full of holes and clods, it was also muddy. She stumbled a few times but avoided falling.

The pair reached Doctor Hackett and Withingham's crew. 'Hi, Doc. So, what have you been able to find out?' Reyes asked. 'Was he a resident of the sidewalk?'

'Could be, but I doubt it,' Doctor Hackett replied. He stood with his gloved hands away from his chest to keep the ashes from touching his shirt. 'I say that because the deceased wore jewelry and a watch. No wallet though. He also has a bullet wound in his head.'

'Shit,' Reyes said. 'There goes my evening.'

Wallace looked at him. 'What's the matter?'

'Nothing,' Reyes said. 'It's nothing.'

'Can we see the victim?' Wallace stepped carefully as she moved closer. All she needed to do now was to twist her already sore ankle to put a capper on the evening.

Dr. Hackett squatted, grabbed the corner of a sheet and pulled it back to uncover a badly charred body that lay face-down, arms by its side. The shirt had been burned off his back, as had the top part of his jeans. The skin where the rubble pile or the cabinet fell on him was less damaged but it was still bad. The hair and ears were gone. He had the remnants of a watch strapped on to his wrist bone and a gold ring on his index finger.

'He died somewhere else,' said Dr. Hackett. 'There was no blood under his body. The bullet cracked his skull right there.' He used his pen as a pointer, indicating a bulge in the top left back of the head of the dead man, suggesting that was where the bullet almost exited his skull. 'The entry wound is here,' he said, pointing to the man's right temple. 'Because of the angle, the man was probably leaning slightly away from whoever shot him. The bullet travelled up, not across.'

'Did you determine if the fire was intentionally set?'

Withingham's assistants stepped closer. Both young. Both blond. Both enthusiastic. *A few more years at this job would drain that from their souls,* Wallace thought.

Hackett signaled the female aide. 'Molly, what did you find so far?'

'There were cans that we suspect held gasoline. Several were found near paint cans. It's unlikely that a construction site would allow

28

gas to be put into cans. It's illegal.' Molly looked at her partner. 'There's a possibility it was arson.'

A shrug of Jason's shoulders brought her quick disclaimer. 'Mr Withingham has the final word, of course.'

'While we're waiting for Withingham and the others to make their way back here,' Dr. Hackett interjected, 'let me touch on a few more things.'

'Go ahead,' said Wallace. She shifted her weight to her left ankle.

'Since beauty and tattoos are both only skin deep, you can scratch finding anything that might identify him. The fire did a good job but there may still be trace evidence around the breastbone area – if there was anything there before, of course. Determining the time of death won't be easy either. The only thing we have is that someone reported the fire about two hours ago. Hmm. Getting closer to three hours now. Since the victim was shot elsewhere and then his body burned here, we're going to struggle with this one a bit.'

Wallace exhaled. 'Keep us in the loop, Doc.'

'We'll run dentals, of course, and we'll get the bullet to ballistics,' Hackett said. 'As soon as we get it out of his brain.'

Hastings and Barclay-Jones walked up the delivery alley. 'What did you find, Doctor?'

29

Barclay-Jones asked.

'Murder and probable arson,' Hackett replied. 'We're waiting for Mr Withingham to confirm a few things.'

'Hastings,' said Wallace, 'we need you to get your guys on the street. Check with their informants, especially the gangs. This may be nothing but an eye for an eye.'

'Will do, but don't count on the gang thing,' Hastings said. 'They normally don't bother to move bodies. They show up shooting and leave the same way. Whatever hits the ground, usually stays on the ground.'

'Detective Wallace,' Barclay-Jones said, 'I know you will be relentless in tracking down the perps who did this. Don't hesitate to call me if you need help.'

'Thanks,' Wallace said.

'Absolutely,' Barclay-Jones said. 'We are behind you all the way.' She turned and wandered away.

'What's with her?' Wallace said. 'She running for office or something?'

'Take a look.' Reyes jerked his thumb to the area behind them.

Wallace turned to see a TV cameraman from one of the state-wide stations filming the scene. She didn't recognize the female reporter with the mic. 'I thought they had all gone home.'

'They must have got wind of a body, so to speak,' Reyes said.

'I'm going back to the front of the building – the long way.'

'I'll meet you there.'

On the slow walk alone, Wallace analyzed the crime. Since the victim died elsewhere, why would someone risk carrying him to the site and then torching the place? Insurance? If the dead man killed himself, his insurance might not pay off. If, on the other hand, he died in a fire, that would be accidental death. If the policy was big enough, that might be worth the risk of being caught carrying a body around LA.

When she reached the front, Reyes was poking through some debris with a pole. He looked up and smiled. 'I told you cutting through the construction site was shorter.'

'At least I didn't sprain an ankle on this route...' Her comment was cut short by the roar of an engine and brakes screeching.

A silver Lexus pulled up to the barricades. A young, angry Asian man leaped from the car. *'Shibal!'* he screamed as he kicked the air. *'Keseki!'* His hands clenched into fists as he shook them over his head and glared at the sky. The man stormed over to confront Marcell.

'Hey. Calm down,' he said.

'Sheba-nom!'

'Seriously. You need to calm down.'

'Wow,' Reyes said. 'Is there a full moon out tonight? What's with him?'

31

'I'll take a wild guess that the owner of this hot pile of rocks has arrived.'

Hastings and the man talked. While the volume went down, the gestures went up. The man waved his arms and hands as his body shook. After a few moments, Hastings turned and pointed toward Wallace and Reyes.

'It doesn't sound like he speaks English and it sure as hell isn't Spanish, either.'

The man stomped over to Wallace and Reyes. Reyes greeted him. 'Me Detective Reyes. That Detective Wallace.' The young man stared in complete confusion. 'You speak English?'

'Fuckin' A, man, who in the hell are you, Charlie Chan? Of course I speak English. My name is Jimmy Jin Moon and I own that goddamn building.' He stared into Reyes' eyes. 'And so help me God, if you say "me so solly", I'll pound rice so far up your ass, sake will come out your nose.'

3

Willy T. slid a cold beer to Kahn. 'Here you go, my friend. How'd that pool go?'

'Not so hot.' Kahn laid a ten-dollar bill on the counter. A hand grabbed his shoulder. Kahn jumped and turned. A well-tanned

32

policeman – Captain judging by his stripes – about 6'2, sandy blond hair, blue eyes.

'Hey, I didn't mean to startle you.' He took the chair next to Kahn, then stuck his hand out. 'Hi. Brian Mangan, Vice. Let me buy you a drink to celebrate our friend Cresner's return.' He nudged the ten spot back toward Kahn and laid a twenty down. 'Take our drinks out of this.'

'You got it,' Willy said.

'Well, that's damn nice of you, except I'm not exactly a friend of Cresner's. I work with a guy who was his partner years ago. Ray Brooks.'

'I know Ray. He's all right.'

'My name's Donald Kahn – Hollywood.' He raised his glass in salute and took a deep draw of the foamy brew.

A stocky guy with a full mustache sidled up to Mangan. 'Captain, I have to run.'

'Already?' Mangan said.

''Fraid so. It's nearly nine.'

'Okay, Sarge. See you tomorrow.'

The man turned to leave, paused and took a second look at Kahn. 'Hey. You look familiar.'

'Don Kahn. I'm Harlen Wagner's partner. You're Krajcek right? From the Super Bowl party.'

He stared at Kahn. 'Wait a minute. Didn't you get wounded a while back?'

'Yeah. Got shot in the afternoon and engaged that night. I'm pretty much recovered from the former, not so much from the latter.'

'Ha! Good to hear it. Well, I have to run. See you guys later.' Krajcek headed for the door.

'Would you excuse me, Captain? I've got some friends sitting back here.'

'Absolutely. You go ahead.'

Kahn hopped off the stool and headed to the table where the other detectives from the squad were seated. He nodded to the others and took a seat.

'I'm not impressed with this whole arrangement,' Siley said. 'You say you tried to call him?'

'I called his house,' Brooks said. 'His wife said a patrol car picked him up about ten minutes before I called. That was about forty minutes ago. It's about a thirty-minute drive from his house to here. Lord knows I made the drive enough times. He has to take the '02 all the way in. Maybe they got stuck in traffic.'

Willy T. had handed the bar off to a kid named Aaron. He seemed too young but, according to Willy T., he knew how to whip up virtually any drink you could name.

Two waitresses had replaced one. Danica and Yvette began moving through the bar. They were both college kids from UCLA working part-time. Danica was a white girl with dark-black hair. Yvette was a light-skinned black girl with red hair. Both were beauties that Wagner wanted to talk into a three-way. Kahn couldn't blame him.

'How's your fiancée?' Coombs asked.

'Angie's fine, thanks.' Kahn glanced around for Wagner and spotted him talking to Kelly Tripucka – one of the female cops he wanted to bang.

'You guys pick a wedding date yet?'

'I don't know. I mean, no. Shit. I just smile and nod. I have no idea what's going on. Angie sort of had things planned out. Then her mom got involved and everything changed. The last I heard, we're looking at spring or fall or one of the other seasons. After much debate, the primary color will be peach, mint-green or maybe ivory. We're renting a hall somewhere unless we hold the wedding outside. We're having cacti instead of flowers.'

'Cacti?'

'Angie's mom wants colored cacti at the church and as center pieces at the reception. I'm trying to imagine my drunken friends doing a conga in a room full of sharp cactus plants.'

'Maybe I'll just send a gift.'

There was a sudden surge of noise by the entrance. Spontaneous applause filled the room, as everyone stood. The word spread: 'Cresner's here.'

35

Kahn was tall enough to see over most of the heads, and saw an old man hobbling down a channel that had opened up in the crowd. So this was the legendary Jerry Cresner. He looked like a scarecrow. His face was gaunt, his short, dark-brown hair had streaks of gray. Although he tried to smile and wave as he passed through the room, each step he took brought the flicker of a grimace as pain cut the deep wrinkles of his face. Before he was shot, the story was that Cresner could run down any suspect. Now he struggled to cross twenty feet of bar-room floor.

Cresner leaned heavily on a sturdy wooden cane. A small replica of a police badge had been embedded near the top. Walking to the chair had apparently drained him of all his strength. He dropped into the seat, took a deep breath, then waved to everyone in the room. 'Thank you all for coming out. I'm glad to be back.'

'You were gone?' someone called out.

Everyone laughed. As some of his closer friends gathered around Cresner's table, he slowly disappeared from Kahn's view.

Kahn turned to Brooks. 'What do you think?'

'He looks like shit.' Brooks scooted his chair away from the table. 'I'm going to go say hello.'

Siley stood as well. 'I'll go with you. You know, I bet he lost fifty pounds.'

36

Captain LaSalle, Cresner's superior officer, had reached his table and officially welcomed him back to duty. 'Jerry, on behalf of all of your friends, we're glad you're back. Your doctor told me that you need to take it easy. I told him you were always good at taking things easy.'

There was applause and a lot of laughing. Kahn stood on his tip-toes. He couldn't see Cresner but LaSalle's face was visible.

'Seriously, we know that you can't do everything yet, but your wife told us that there is one thing you can still do very well.'

The bar filled with appropriate laughter. Captain LaSalle looked around, feigning ignorance. 'What?' he smiled. 'I don't know what they're laughing at, Jerry. All I know is that Mary said you've been practicing a lot for the last three months.'

More laughter.

'Somebody had to help him exercise those hips,' the same joker as before shouted out.

Even more laughs.

'Come on people,' Captain LaSalle said. 'I was talking about watching TV. Mary said Jerry's been doing a lot of that. Since football season is upon us,' he said, 'what better way to relax than to sit in that recliner of yours, eating a slice of Mary's world-famous orange-apple pie and watching the games on...'

One of the officers pushed a cart into the

37

circle near the table where Cresner sat, a blanket covering something on top. With everyone's eyes on the prize, Captain LaSalle finished his statement '…your brand new plasma TV.' Simultaneously, the officer pulled the blanket.

Kahn couldn't see him but he heard the surprise in Cresner's voice. 'Are you kidding me? Damn. That's really great.'

A chant of 'Speech! Speech!' filled the room.

With help, Cresner rose and turned slightly, first one way, then another. 'I didn't plan a speech. I guess if I had known that getting laid up for three months would get me a new TV, I'd have done it years ago!' he said. 'Seriously guys, thanks for all the cards and calls. Your support proves once again the camaraderie of the boys in blue. Thanks, everyone.'

He sat to a round of applause. Danica pushed another cart with a welcome back cake on it. She led the singing of 'For He's a Jolly Good Fellow'.

'Cresner's not going back on the street is he?' Coombs asked. 'The man can barely stand, let alone walk or run.'

'Captain Siley said that he'll be doing nothing but desk duty until the doctors clear him,' said Albanese. 'From the looks of him, that won't be for a long time.'

Brooks and Siley returned to the table.

Brooks gulped his gin and tonic. 'Whew. That was rough, seeing him in that shape.'

'I still don't know who approved his return.' Captain Siley poked at the slice of lime in his glass with the swizzle stick. 'Guys, I have to get going. Margie and some of the neighbors play cards every other week. There's a widower from two doors along makes passes at my wife. If I don't get there by nine-thirty, I think she may go off with him.'

Kahn bought another round. Brooks raised his glass. 'Here's to old friends and their hopes and dreams.'

'Wait for me,' Coombs said. She grabbed her drink. Everyone clinked glasses. 'To old friends.'

Brooks stood up, drink in hand. 'Time for me to go home. I'm going to say goodbye to Cresner. I'll see you all tomorrow.'

'I think I've had enough, too,' Coombs said. 'By the way, Sal called. He and Wallace have an arson and a homicide.'

'Long night for them.' Albanese said. 'But not for me. How about you Don?'

'Angie has parent–teacher meetings to-night. I think I'll hang out here for a little while.'

Kahn checked the room, looking for Wagner. It didn't surprise him to see his partner pressing close to Kelly Tripucka again, the rookie from Sergeant Blaylock's group. Kahn hoped for Wagner's sake that

39

the attraction was mutual.

It wasn't that long ago that he and Wagner would have been tag-teaming, trying to get girls like Danica and Yvette to meet them after work. Now, with Angie in his life, his partner was left to his own devices. The poor bastard would probably have to pick between one of the numerous gorgeous girls here tonight.

Tripucka suddenly shouted out. 'Who do you think you are?'

Blaylock immediately stepped in. 'What the hell is going on here?'

Wagner was gesturing wildly, but Kahn couldn't hear what he was saying. Most likely he was whipping out the standard excuses. *No harm, no foul. She misunderstood me. I didn't know that she was married, engaged, spoken for, your daughter, a nun...*

Kahn laughed. Angie looked better all the time. Cresner got up. He lost his balance momentarily as the cane slipped, and then hobbled slowly toward the door to the men's room.

Kahn watched him make his way across the bar. He remembered being shot and how scared he was and how he was afraid his insides wouldn't heal. He had been very lucky, unlike poor Cresner, who was obviously still having problems. Still, at least he got a TV out of it.

4

Reyes let Johnny Jin Moon circle around the outer perimeter of the site. He'd explained their initial suspicions about the homicide and arson.

'That's crazy talk. Why would someone burn down my building?'

Jesus, thought Reyes. *This guy needs to look at his priorities.*

'We were hoping you could answer that. And maybe give us an idea about who the body might be.'

'None of my employees should have been in there. The contractor was going to be painting and I told everyone to go home. Too many fumes.'

'Can you account for all of your people?'

'No. I'll check on them right away.'

'We'd appreciate it if you could let us have a list of their names and addresses as soon as possible, so we can carry out our own checks.'

'Sure, sure.'

'We have a lot of questions as well, Mr Moon,' Reyes said. 'Can you tell us where you were this afternoon?'

'I had a late lunch meeting with the producer, director and one of the money men behind *Saturnsaurus.*' He winced. 'All their equipment was in there. I hope to hell it was insured.'

'Whose equipment are you referring to?'

'The people who are filming *Saturnsaurus – The Invasion.*'

'You're going to have to be a little more specific, Mr Moon,' Wallace said. 'It's nearly ten now. Did you meet with these people all afternoon?'

Moon glanced at Wallace, then Reyes. 'Sort of.'

'Could you elaborate?'

'I was helping select cast members. You know, select?'

'We're going to need names of the people you met with today.' Reyes tapped his tablet. 'For the record.'

'You'll have to talk to the casting agent for the names. And, uh, I'd appreciate it if you didn't tell my wife where I was. You know?'

'Uh-huh. Do you know anyone who might have a reason to burn down your place?'

Reyes glanced over and waved as the last firefighters packed up. 'Do you owe anybody money?'

'Everybody has a man to pay, detective,' said Moon. 'But the answer to your real question is "no". I don't have any problem debts.'

'Maybe you did something that pissed somebody off?' Wallace asked. 'Your local

42

gang-bangers perhaps?'

'I haven't had trouble with anybody around here.' His hand suddenly shot into his pocket. Reyes tensed, but Moon whipped out his business card holder. 'Here,' he said. 'Here's my card. I have to go, gentlemen. I have to call my employees and my insurance agent. And the folks at TerrorTory Productions. God, maybe the man in there is one of their people. Or the construction company's. Shit. I had better call them as well.'

'TerrorTory Productions?' Wallace said. 'Who are they?

'They're a small independent – aren't they all – specializing in space horror movies. The owner is a lady named Tory Moa.'

'And who is your construction company?' Reyes asked.

'Pearl. Hold on.' Moon pulled the number up on his cell phone screen and gave it to Reyes. They took the number for Tory Moa also.

'Remember to call us when you finish checking on your employees,' said Reyes.

Moon nodded and headed for his car. 'I hope you find the bastards who did this.'

'We'll do our best,' Reyes said, but Moon didn't wait to hear any more. He closed the door and was already making a call as he pulled away.

Goodnight, Moon. Reyes smiled. Nando had loved that story at bedtime.

He turned to Wallace. 'What do you think?'

'I don't think he had anything to do with either the fire or the killing. The body bothered him only because he thought that it might have been someone working on his building. All of his other concerns seemed to be about his staff, getting the film back on track and getting his business up and running.'

'It could be that he burned it down for the insurance.'

'Yeah, I suppose, but it's not unusual to make a call to your insurance company after something like this. If we're not out of here within the next hour, I fully expect we'll see his agent down here taking pictures, nosing around, trying to figure out a way that they don't have to pay Moon off.'

'Hey, guys,' Hastings said. 'The meat wagon is here. They've got the body loaded. Doc wants to know if you need anything before he leaves.'

'No,' Wallace said. 'Tell them if they get anything important in the next hour or so, we'll be at the station. Otherwise one of us will call in the morning. We'll need a patrol to keep an eye on this overnight. We may be back tomorrow if we have some more to go on.'

'Gotcha,' Hastings said. His thumb depressed the button on his radio. 'Hey, Marcell. Wrap it with a bow. Tell the boys in

44

the back that they can go.'

Reyes checked his watch. 'Let's go back and file our report.'

'You seem in a hurry.'

'I kind of had plans tonight.'

'Your job getting in the way of your life again?'

'Sure does seem to happen a lot, doesn't it?'

'Yeah, it does. Times two in my case.'

Reyes was surprised by the answer but before he could say another word, a titanium-colored Dodge Charger screeched to a halt next to Hasting's police car. A pudgy man who, in the right outfit, could pass for a fat Elvis imitator, stepped out of the car. He slammed his palm on the hood of his car over and over again while screaming at the top of his lungs. 'Goddamn that mother-fucking son of a bitch. I'll kill the bastard.'

'I guess I don't have to ask him if he speaks English,' Reyes said.

'Who's in charge here?' the man yelled. 'I need to talk to the man in charge.'

'I'm the woman in charge,' said Wallace. 'My name's Detective Wallace. This is Detective Reyes.'

'My name is Sonny Giordano with Pearl Construction. This is ... was ... my build.'

'So, you're Moon's contractor? What can we do for you?'

'Not a damn thing, but I can tell you who

45

the prick is that burned this building down. It was that scum-sucking Sam Davey, that's who.'

Reyes jotted down the name. 'You think this fire was intentionally set?'

'Hell, yes I do.'

'Who is this Sam Davey and why would he want to burn down your building?'

'He's a competitor, you know? Sphinx Construction. He was really pissed when he didn't get this job. He called me a crook.'

'So he torched the place? That's a bit extreme, don't you think?'

'Extreme? The son of a bitch threatened me. As soon as he found out that I was awarded phase two of the job, he said he'd get me and my brother-in-law.'

'Mr Giordano,' Wallace said, 'calm down. Are you saying this is about business?'

Reyes noticed that she hadn't mentioned the more pressing concern of the body.

'Yeah, pretty much. Our bids for the film build were almost identical. Since I was already on site with the expansion project, it was more efficient to let me finish both jobs.'

'So,' Reyes said, 'that would piss him off so much that he'd burn the place down?'

'I'd say that was for him to answer. I'll tell you what I do know, though. The only reason he has the balls to do this shit is because my brother-in-law isn't around.'

'Why wouldn't he – you know – burn down

the building if your brother-in-law was around?'

'Because my brother-in-law would kick his ass.'

'I see. We may need to talk to your brother-in-law later. Can you give me his name?'

'Yeah, sure. His name is Bart Pearl. He owns the company.'

'I think I should let you know that we found a body in the fire.'

'What?' Giordano sputtered, his face drained, a sick ashen color replacing the pink in his cheeks.

'Who was it? I mean ... it couldn't have been Bart. He's in jail. Incarcerated.'

'We don't have any identification on the victim yet other than it was a male. Do you have any guesses who the deceased might be?' Reyes asked.

He shook his head. 'I have no idea. None.' He index and middle finger pressed against his lips. 'Damn. Did you want me to see if I can identify the person?'

'We've already moved the remains,' Reyes said. 'Not that it would have done much good. You understand?'

'Oh. Right.'

'Could you tell us where you were this afternoon? Say from twelve on?'

'Me? I'm one of the victims and you cops try to make me the bad guy? Unbelievable. Fine. I think I can fill in the blanks. I had lunch at the Italian place near my office in WeHo. It's called The Rubicon on North Crescent Heights.' He paused, snapped his fingers and said, 'Oh yeah, I know. I stopped and bought a pack of Rolaids at Arnies. A block over from the restaurant. Then I went back to the office. I was there until around four. Then I went home.'

'Did you have lunch with anybody who could confirm that you were this restaurant?' Reyes asked.

'The owner, Mario Bertelli is his name. He's an old friend. He sat with me for a while.'

'I assume there were people in your office who will testify to your presence?'

'My secretary sits about ten feet away. She'll tell you.'

'How about at home?'

'My wife.'

'I bet your dog was there too.'

'My dog? What the hell is that supposed to mean?'

'Only that you seem to be surrounded by a lot of loyal friends, Mr Giordano. How fortunate for you. You can go now.' Reyes was hoping that the hint of disbelief would bring an exaggerated response – one that might accidentally reveal more than Giordano wanted. He refused the bait.

'Yeah. Maybe I will go home now. It doesn't look like I can do much here.'

'Not tonight. It's officially a crime scene now, I'm afraid. We're looking at arson. Maybe murder. Hopefully we'll be able to let you rummage around some time tomorrow, but I can't promise.'

'Okay. I guess I'll go, then.' He backed away a few steps. 'You go check Davey out. That's who did this.'

They watched him drive off. Reyes looked at Wallace. 'I'm sorry, but I gotta say it.'

Wallace looked confused. 'Say what?'

'Elvis has left the building.'

5

Wallace was hungry and tired but she was home. She stepped inside the front door and kicked off her shoes. 'Oooh. That feels so good I feel guilty not paying for the pleasure.' Her ankle was still sore but didn't look swollen. If she kept it elevated, it would be fine by morning.

'David?' she called softly. No answer. *Maybe he's gone to bed already.*

She took her suit jacket off and threw it over a hook on the tree. Quietly, she moved down the hall toward their bedroom. Phil sure as hell didn't want to wake David if he had managed to fall asleep. He had been in a foul mood lately and said it was due to lack of sleep. Most mornings she'd wake to discover that his side of the bed was empty, and she'd find him sprawled on the couch or the recliner, with the television on. When she asked him what was wrong, he blew her off with a litany of excuses. Headache. Dinner didn't settle well. Too hot. She didn't think it was any of those things. For a while she wondered if it might be another woman, but there weren't any signs of that, either. Whatever it was, she couldn't put a finger on it and that bugged the hell out of her.

There was a light coming from under the door of the office. They had planned on making it the baby's room at one time, but after a while, it had become their home office. That was twenty years ago and, in Wallace's opinion, that was part of the trouble they were having. But David's problems seemed more recent, more intense. She pressed her ear against the door. No noise. Maybe he had fallen asleep using the computer.

As quietly as she could, she turned the knob and opened the door. David was awake and furiously reading the open page on his laptop. His hand cupped the mouse and scrolled down the page. David reached for a tablet and made a note and when he did, Phil caught a glimpse of some kind of spreadsheet. Then he spotted her standing silently in the doorway.

'Holy...' David said, with a start. 'Don't sneak up on a guy like that.'

'I'm sorry. I thought you were asleep. What are you doing?'

David turned to the computer and minimized the window. 'Nothing. I'm catching up on some shit for work is all.'

'FID has you taking work home now?' She stared at her husband. He appeared confused. No, no, not confused. He looked in pain.

'It's nothing. The major asked me to lend him a hand cleaning up some stuff.'

'Really?'

'What's that mean? Don't you trust me?'

'Hey. What's the matter with you? Of course I trust you. I was only asking.'

David's chin dropped to his chest. Slowly, he raised his head with a look of sad frustration. 'I'm sorry. It's nothing.'

'Okay, it's nothing. Let's change the subject. What did you have for dinner?'

'I stopped and got a crab roll on the way home.'

'Swell.'

'Want me to run out and get you something?'

'No. You go ahead doing "nothing". I'm going to go scrounge up something to eat and watch a little TV.'

Phil stepped from the room and closed the door behind her. She tried to picture what

51

had been revealed during her brief glimpse of the computer screen.

Phil poured enough water for a single cup of coffee into her coffee machine and switched it on. She heard the familiar gurgle as it started heating the water. While it brewed, she took out some peach yogurt, put a handful of granola into it and headed for the living-room. She found the remote on the table next to David's chair. The couch seemed to be the most inviting space to rest, to stretch and to put her tired feet up. She sat, sighed, and took a spoonful of what was passing for dinner that night. Mindlessly, she began flipping through the channels.

What in the hell could be so damned important about a spreadsheet that David would want to hide it from me? Was that really Force Investigation work?

The ten o'clock news was on, and they were covering the fire. Standard stuff. A reporter – Muffet McKnight – with the fire behind her. *Back to you Celeste.* Wallace chuckled a little. The media must have shown up when the fire was at its zenith. They came, got their shots, did an interview with Hastings, then left once the building fell in on itself. By the time Wallace had arrived, they were all off in search of other tragedies, except for that newbie from Fox. She'd been lucky not having to wade through that school of piranhas.

Wallace finished her yogurt while the news anchor droned on about obese children, a gun brought to a local elementary school and the governor promising to lower taxes if he was re-elected. She returned to the kitchen and poured herself a cup of coffee, grabbed two Oreos from the cookie jar and went back to the couch.

She clicked 'up' on the remote and saw Humphrey Bogart's handsome face. The Classic Movie Channel was her secret guilty pleasure and *Casablanca* was at the top of her list of favorites.

'Monsieur Rick, what kind of a man is Captain Renault?'

'Oh, he's just like any other man, only more so.'

Wallace heard the door to the study open. She turned slightly and watched David disappear down the hall. The light from the bathroom was followed by the sound of the door closing. Instinct took over. She stood, put her coffee and second cookie on the table and hobbled hurriedly down the hall. She peeked into the study. The laptop sat open.

She stood in the doorway, torn between curiosity and a vow. 'David?'

'In the bathroom.'

'If you're done working for tonight, *Casablanca's* on.'

'I'll be out in a minute.'

Wallace took a last look at the screen. *What am I doing here?* She trusted David, didn't she?

She returned to Bogie. A few minutes passed and David entered the room, carrying his laptop. He sat in his chair and opened his computer. He clicked a few buttons and the glow reflected on his face.

'Can you mute that, please?'

She pushed mute and dropped the remote on the couch next to her. 'What's up?'

'Look, things might get a little rough in the coming days. I'm not supposed to be letting this out to anyone but...'

'Don't you think you can trust me?'

'It's not my doing. I've been ordered to keep this investigation quiet but...'

'But what? Come on. You know I'm not big on melodrama. Could you cut to the chase and tell me what's on your mind?'

He stared at her as if, perhaps, he was reconsidering what he had said.

'Look, if you don't want to tell me, don't. Me and Bogie got a thing going on.'

David said nothing. Phil reached for the remote.

'The District Attorney thinks we have a bad cop or two in the department.'

Wallace swallowed hard and withdrew her hand. 'What? Why do they think that?'

'I can't tell you everything yet, but this investigation has been going on for months. Now the pressure is on to wrap it up.'

'Why didn't you tell me this before? You've

had investigations in the past and you've always shared them with me.' Wallace paused, her head tilted slightly back. Her eyes focused on the slowly turning overhead fan. 'Aw shit!' She paused. 'You think something's rotten in the Hollywood, don't you?'

'And Wilshire.'

'Who?'

David shook his head.

'What, then? Can you tell me what the cops did?'

'The District Attorney thinks someone is dealing in stolen weapons.'

'Guns?'

'Pieces the police confiscated and scheduled for destruction are showing up on the street. Look, I've probably said way more than I should have. I didn't want you getting caught flatfooted on this. It's been tearing me up. I didn't know what the hell to do. Soon we're gonna have to come out with this and your buddies are going to wonder which side you're on.'

'Which side I'm on? So you're saying that some of the cops they're looking at are in my squad? My detective squad?'

'I can't say. I could be in deep shit if word gets out on this before we move. You have to keep it to yourself.'

She gave him one of those looks but David closed his computer. 'I shouldn't have told you. They specifically said not to tell you. But

I couldn't...' He looked at her with the sad eyes of a puppy that had pissed on the carpet.

'Don't let it worry you. I won't let it leak, I promise.'

'Thanks. I'm really tired. Do you want to go to bed?'

'You go ahead. I've had a rough one today myself. I'm going to unwind a little with Bogie before I hit the sack.'

'Fair enough,' David said. He rose and crossed the room. He stopped momentarily and looked at her. 'I love you.'

Phil nodded. 'Thanks for telling me.'

David smiled weakly. 'Goodnight.'

'Goodnight.' Wallace waited until she heard the bedroom door close. Selling guns? Who the hell would be stupid enough to do something like that? She dunked her Oreo into the lukewarm coffee. Wagner? Had that dumb idiot gotten himself involved in something stupid? No. Not likely. He was a pain in the ass sometimes, but he was honest. Shit.

I was probably better off not knowing. What's that old saying? A little knowledge is a dangerous thing.

Phil clicked the volume. She mouthed the dialogue along with Bogie.

'*I remember every detail. The Germans wore gray, you wore blue.*'

She sipped her coffee, wishing she was at the bar in Rick's Americain instead of sitting here worrying about David and his damned investigation. No one on the squad would do anything crooked. She was sure.

Ninety-nine per cent.

Wallace finished her Oreo and washed it down with another sip. In a few minutes she was back in Casablanca with Bogie and Bergman where nothing made sense and yet, everything seemed perfectly logical.

6

'Everybody can relax, I'm here,' Wagner said. Kahn looked up and saw his partner at the door, holding up a grease-stained sack. 'Anybody want a doughnut?'

'Where they from?' shouted Emilio Albanese.

'What the hell difference does that make?'

'If they're from Stan's, I'll take one.'

'Well, they ain't from Stan's. You want one anyway?'

'Got a gooseberry-filled?'

'I'll take that as a "no". Gooseberry? Christ.' Wagner walked down the center aisle of the Pit. 'Anyone, anyone? Where are Phil and our Mexican friend?'

'They wanted to catch a suspect early,' said Coombs.

Wagner reached Kahn's cubicle and stuck

the bag over the wall. 'Doughnut, partner? Sorry I couldn't find one that Angie would approve of but they didn't have any low fat, no sugar, tofu ones. Go figure, huh?'

'Jesus, Harlen,' Kahn said. 'You look like you slept in a pile of donkey shit.'

Wagner was unshaven. His tie was tangled and there were stains on his shirt collar. It was pretty sad display and that was only the parts Kahn could see. 'We've got a little morning duty to perform.'

Wagner stepped around and took a seat next to Kahn's desk. He took out a plain cake doughnut, showed it to Kahn and took a bite. 'Gotta soak up the beer.' He slapped his stomach. 'I'm probably going to need a dozen of 'em.'

'You didn't make it home last night, I assume.'

Wagner brushed a few crumbs from his tie and shirt. 'I made it to somebody's home. I just can't remember whose.'

'You can fill me in some other time. Seeing as it's 8.20, I started work without you. I hope you don't mind.'

'Pussywhipped.'

'What?'

'Angie is turning you into a eunuch. So I'm twenty minutes late. Big fucking deal. You're as bad as Albanese with his fuckin' gooseberry doughnut shit, except he doesn't have a woman to blame it on.'

58

'Moving right along. I got a call from Ren Takata over at Narcotics about twenty minutes ago. Do you remember the Tarántula Azul Airlines drug bust?

'Sort of.' A spray of partially chewed doughnut spewed over the desk. 'I'm a little foggy this morning.' Wagner crimped the top of the doughnut sack and dropped it on Kahn's desk. 'Weren't the guys in charge of that airline running a narcotics smuggling ring? They were bringing the drugs in on their own planes.'

'Right. Narcotics swept up most everyone from the airline's LAX offices. They didn't do quite as well in the South American or Mexican units, but they got some of those guys, too. In the final tally, they got enough of the players to cripple the operation.'

'Okay, so what's up?' Wagner picked up the photograph of Kahn's fiancée with his greasy fingers. Kahn reached over, took the photo and placed it back on the desk.

'When their raid went down, they missed one of their main targets. The ex-gang lord, Jesus Santana.'

'I remember that shithead. He was like the king of some Hispanic gang in LA.'

'Yeah, El Cuervos to be exact. The Crows. Nasty group. He worked out quite an arrangement. He had several Latino gangs buying the Tarántula Azul drugs from him.'

'Didn't he get the hell out of dodge two

steps ahead of the hounds?'

'He headed to Mexico at the first sign of trouble. However, Takata said someone spotted him at his mother's house in South LA yesterday.'

'South LA? Goddamn it, are you getting PC now on top of everything else? Come on partner, call a pig a pig.'

'Okay, okay. South Central. That better?'

'It is what it is.'

'In any case, Santana's got a sheet as long as your arm, including an outstanding murder charge from 2005. Narcotics is asking for an assist on this one.'

'Then what are we waiting for? Give me two minutes to refill my cup and I'll meet you at the car.'

Kahn grabbed a few notes off of his desk and headed for the car. He climbed in, started it up, then glanced at his notes for the proper spelling of Santana's mother's name. As he typed 'Santana, Esmerelda' into the computer, Wagner joined him.

'Hey, partner,' Wagner said. He put his travel-mug into the cup-holder, buckled his seat belt and immediately lit a cigarette. 'Let's do it.' He offered the pack to Kahn.

Kahn lit up as he pulled out of the division's parking lot and headed south on Wilcox to Sunset.

'What part of paradise are we headed to?'

'Right in the middle of Inglewood.' He

checked the computer screen. 'South Le Brea to be exact. We should be there about 9.30.' Kahn flipped his ash out the window as he turned south on Highland. 'So, what did Blaylock have to say about you hitting on his rookie?'

'That was such bullshit. I think he's getting some of that. She was fine with everything and then she saw Blaylock and she went all ape-shit on me.'

'How much trouble are you in?'

'None. Everything's cool.'

Wagner spun the computer and typed in 'Santana, Jesus'. His file appeared on the screen. 'I want to see what this guy looks like.' He clicked 'Photo' and a four by five jpeg popped up. The headshot of a young man filled the screen. 'Hell, he actually isn't bad looking. Only twenty-nine.'

'He didn't strike me as your type. I mean, you do know he's a Mexican, right?'

'Up yours. I figured he would have a pockmarked face and greasy hair. Shit like that. He looks kind of respectable.'

'Except he pushes drugs and isn't picky about who he pulls the trigger on.'

'Hey. All I'm saying is that he ain't ugly, okay?'

Traffic slowed for a bus-motorcycle accident at Melrose and Highland. A few bystanders were taking pictures with their cell phones while the police systematically funneled traffic around the broken parts. The EMTs worked frantically as they moved the rider toward the ambulance. *Poor bastard.*

Kahn gripped the wheel at the ten and two position and stared at the speedometer. 'I know you don't like Angie.'

Wagner's body jerked around. 'What? That's not true. She's got a nice ass and all, but you'll never convince me that tofu is a food. But I don't have to eat that shit. You do. If that's good enough for you, then go for it.'

'I'm having trouble adjusting to the food rules myself,' said Kahn, keeping his eyes on the road. 'I still think it's worth it, though.'

'So you're happy without meat and cigarettes?'

'I still cheat.' He held up his cigarette.

'And what about chasing women and getting drunk? Take last night, for instance...'

'That was getting old,' Kahn said, cutting off Wagner's tale of conquest. 'I really don't miss either, most of the time anyway.'

Wagner shrugged.

Kahn flipped his cigarette out of the window. 'You're still in as my best man, right?'

'Fuck, yes. Did you really think I'd back out because your bride-to-be doesn't eat meat?'

'Yeah. I guess.'

The accident added almost twenty minutes to the drive time. Kahn slowed as he passed the address. He leaned over and eyed the house. One story, gray shingles. Detached one-car garage. No one visible. 'See anything?'

'No. Mama must still live here, though. There's a small veggie garden along the fence. Looked like lace curtains on the front window.'

Kahn pulled the car around the corner and stopped. He picked up the radio. 'Adam Zero-Zero-Five. We are Code Six at 721 South Le Brea.'

'Ready?' Wagner grabbed the door handle and was out of the car.

Kahn stepped into the street, gave the neighborhood a once-over and then joined Wagner.

'Front or back?'

'Let's check around outside first.'

Wagner walked two steps ahead of him down the gravel driveway. Kahn felt as though they were being watched. He scanned the windows on the side of the house, looking for any sign of movement – the ruffle of a curtain, a shadow, the glint of a gun-barrel. He wasn't quite as sure of himself as he was before he had been shot. Nearly two months of desk duty had dulled his instincts, slowed his reflexes. He was rusty.

Voices.

Kahn stopped and looked at his partner. Wagner pointed toward the garage, signaled to move forward. Kahn nodded and as silently as he could, walked to the left as Wag-

63

ner moved right. There were six frosted windows in the garage door. Two were boarded up. No one was visible through the other four, despite there obviously being someone inside.

Each step he took in the driveway sounded as though he was crushing a hundred grasshoppers underfoot. Surely they could hear the noise inside the garage? Or was it because the blood was pounding in his skull that everything sounded more intense?

Calm down. It could be Santana's mother in the garage getting a screwdriver.

Kahn rested his left shoulder against the front of the garage. Wagner assumed a mirrored position on the other side. He waved, and then gestured that he was going to lift the door while Kahn provided cover. Kahn nodded.

Wagner held up three fingers for the silent countdown. Three. Two.

The glass in the window closest to Wagner's head exploded. A bullet whined its way past him, carrying shards of broken glass with it and slammed into the house.

'Shit,' Wagner yelled, as he spun away and dove into the backyard.

'Police! Drop your weapons!' Kahn yelled.

Another shell tore through the door near Kahn's groin. He stumbled back and around the side of the garage. He squeezed his radio mic. 'This is three-oh-three. Shots fired.

Requesting backup. Repeat. Three-oh-three reporting a nine-nine-niner.'

The door was thrown open and four men ran from the garage, howling, cursing, shouting. One waved a gun as they barreled down the driveway. He turned and fired. Kahn rolled back along the outside wall of the garage.

'Police!' Kahn yelled. He took aim on the last man, low, at the legs, but Wagner stumbled into his line of fire.

'Police, you sons of bitches. Stop!'

One man bolted to the left, one ran straight and entered an alley, two more, including the gunman, headed right. Wagner gave chase to the guy in the alley.

Kahn reached the street, hesitated. No one was visible to the left and to the right, only one man was still in sight. *I guess he's mine.* Kahn called in again. 'Three-oh-three. In foot pursuit of Hispanic male. White T. Jeans. Running west on Regent.'

He had covered only a block when a squad car pulled out, lights flashing and took up the chase. Kahn stopped. He was puffing pretty bad. Out of shape. Besides, the squad was closer than he was. They could have him.

Kahn hurried back to catch up with his partner. He crushed the talk button on his radio. 'Wagner. Where you at? I'm entering the alley now.'

'Block and a half down the alley moving

65

south.' Wagner said. 'I had him for a second but the little greaser got away.'

'You still have a visual?'

'He's here somewhere. I think he's in the backyard of this house.'

Kahn ran down the alley. He saw a white object fly from the left and strike Wagner, who only had enough time to put up his right arm to deflect it. A flower pot. Dirt, glass and flowers exploded across the road.

'Goddamn it!' he screamed, staggered back and fell to the street. 'Mother-fucker!'

Kahn raced up in time to see a matching flower pot come hurtling at Wagner from a back porch. This time he jumped aside. The pot shattered in the street, scattering begonias.

Wagner burst through the back gate and raced toward a young Latino man on the porch. The man jammed his hand into his jeans pocket.

'He's going for a weapon!' Kahn shouted.

The Latino took two steps down the back stairs. Wagner launched himself into the man's chest. They stumbled backward, and toppled into the steps. Wagner was thrown off and the Latino rolled over and pushed himself with his right arm from the horizontal to a near-seated position. Kahn kicked his right forearm as hard as he could.

The arm snapped. *'Santa Maria!'* the man screamed. *'Mi brazo! Mi brazo!'*

Wagner gasped for air as he struggled for his cuffs. 'Don't ... let him ... get into ... his pocket.'

'Don't worry. I broke his fucking arm,' Kahn said. 'You okay?'

Wagner rolled on to his back, pointed at his chest as he sucked in air. 'Smoking ... kills.'

'Take it easy. Everything's cool.' Kahn reported the arrest of the suspect. 'We have one of the four. He was injured resisting. Need an ambulance. We're in the alley across from the South Le Brea address.'

'That ain't Santana,' said Wagner, now on his haunches.

'No shit.'

Wagner held his ribs as he took a deep breath. 'He matched the description.'

'They all matched the description.' Kahn squatted next to the groaning man and patted his front jean pockets. 'What's your name?'

'You broke my arm, mother-fucker.'

Kahn stood over the fallen youth. 'If you don't tell me your name right now, I'm going to break the other.'

The young man's tear-filled eyes widened. 'Alejandro López.'

'Okay, don't start crying now, tough guy,' Kahn said. 'Who else was in the garage with you? I need names. Was one of them named Santana? Jesus Santana?'

López shook his head. *'No sé.'* He groaned

and clutched his upper arm tighter as Kahn pulled a house key from López's front pocket. 'A key.' He held it up and showed Wagner.

Wagner squatted over him and frowned. 'Come on, don't try to be the hero. You guys shot at cops. You're in a world of hurt. Help yourself out. Tell me who had the gun, ya dumb shit.'

'I don't know!' he yelled. He stared through watery eyes at Wagner. 'I don't know. I wasn't there. Get me an ambulance. You broke my arm.'

'I chased your ass down here, Alejandro, so that bullshit isn't going to fly. Now, how about you tell me where you live?'

The suspect moaned. 'Here. I live here. That's my house key.'

'I'll bet.' Wagner eased Kahn aside and rolled the man over. He screamed but Wagner didn't stop until he had found the guy's wallet.

'Okay, let's see what this might tell us.' Wagner searched through the wallet for ID. 'No driver's license. No green card. Six bucks. I guess you're not dealing. Oh, here's something.' Wagner pulled out a photo ID, then rolled his eyes. 'Crap.'

'What is it?' Kahn asked.

'Here.'

Kahn looked at the laminated ID. 'Hey, Alejandro?'

Lopez's face was scrunched up in pain. 'What?'

'This is a high school ID. Is this you?'

'Who the fuck do you think it is?'

'He's fifteen. And he lives here.'

'Yup,' Wagner said. 'And he sure as hell ain't Santana.'

Kahn sighed. 'The arrest report is going to be fun.'

Wagner nodded. He looked at his own arm, held it up for Kahn. There were several scratches and a good sized red welt a few inches below his elbow. 'And unfortunately partner, it looks like my writing arm is going to be out of action for a few hours.'

7

Reyes parked the car in front of the Davey home on South Weverly. 'Nice neighborhood. Near Wilshire, but quiet.'

Wallace checked in the wing mirror, her hand on the door. 'Quiet at half past eight in the morning. Let's go see how evil this Sam Davey really is.'

'How's your ankle?'

'It's fine.' She'd kept ice on it until the end of the movie, and popped a couple of painkillers that morning. She looked at the

Davey's house. The background check they ran suggested Davey made serious money but the house, though large, was certainly not overwhelming. Unpretentious. Simple. Light-gray fieldstone. White trim. Small, neat yard. Very conservative.

Reyes rang the bell. A pale, small man with sandy hair opened the door. He was wearing a bathrobe. 'Yes?'

Wallace held her ID out for him to see. 'I'm Detective Wallace. This is Detective Reyes.'

'Ah. You're the ones who called this morning. I'm Sam Davey. I was just about to throw on some clothes. Come in.' He stepped aside and gestured for them to enter.

Wallace and Reyes were shown into the living-room. Neatly decorated with sturdy furniture from someplace like Sears.

'This is my wife, Janet,' Davey said.

Wallace looked over the attractive woman. She had short, brown hair and wore designer jeans and a raspberry-colored three-quarter length sleeve shirt. Her wing chair – it had to be her chair that she stood in front of – was covered with a muted rose fabric. She wore a lot of gold jewelry; Wallace counted five bangles on her wrists and noted heavy, looped earrings. Cigarette smoke curled up from the ashtray. A glass of cola or iced tea sat on the end table on a ceramic coaster. Mrs Davey nervously wrung her hands as she greeted the officers.

'Hello,' she said. 'Would you like a cup of coffee or tea?'

'Coffee if you have it,' Wallace said. 'Thank you.'

'I'm good,' Reyes said.

'Excuse me,' Janet said, scurrying out of the room.

'Have a seat,' Davey said. He sat in a recliner. Wallace took out a notebook, dropped it on to the coffee table and took a seat on the dark-brown sofa. Reyes stood off to the side studying the photographs and artwork hanging on the walls.

'Are these buildings here in the photos ones your company built?'

'Yes. Most of them. There are a couple of famous buildings like the Empire State under construction.' Davey felt his robe pocket, looked to the chair where his wife had been seated. 'Do you see a pack of cigarettes over there?'

'Yeah,' Reyes picked up a pack of Montelairs and handed them to Davey.

'Thanks. So, what can I do for you?' He lit his cigarette with a milk porcelain table lighter.

'Like I told you over the phone, there was a fire at the Green Cheese Entertainment building.'

'Damn shame, but why are you here?'

'Your company, that's Sphinx Construction right?'

71

'Yes.'

'Did you bid on the Green Cheese project?'

'I bid on Phase Two – the film set. I passed on the expansion project.'

'Why did you choose not bid to on that part of it?'

'For years my company focused on commercial construction. It's still the major part of our business. However, a few years back, we began moving in a new direction, focusing on constructing film sets. We're slowly building that division to be self-sufficient.'

'Really? So you would drop commercial construction all together?'

'We would keep our finger in the pie. Who knows what tomorrow might bring? Maybe these independent film companies all fold tomorrow. Then what? But for now, there's money to be had.'

'Is there enough money there for you and your competitors?'

'It's a booming business right now. See, in the old days in Hollywood, it used to be only the major studios that needed that kind of work done. But today, with all the new technology, almost anybody can make a picture. Those that get a few bucks together have sets built.'

'I didn't know that,' Wallace said. 'And you say there's enough work there to keep your company in the black?'

'Let me tell you something. My family has been in the construction business here in LA for three generations. You survive by knowing the market and adapting to it.'

'Here's the coffee,' Janet said, carrying in a tray.

The offer of a simple cup of coffee had turned into a performance. Mrs Davey carried a silver coffee pot, creamer and sugar bowl on a silver tray and set it on the table. She poured coffee for Wallace. 'Cream, sugar, Sweet'N Low or hazelnut Cremora?'

Wallace declined. 'Black is fine.'

Mrs Davey put a small almond cookie on the edge of the saucer and handed it to her.

'Are you sure you won't have something?' She smiled at Reyes while she prepared a cup for her husband.

'The coffee does smell good,' Reyes said. 'Okay, sure. Just a splash of cream, please.' He took a seat on the sofa next to Wallace. Janet Davey poured another cup, added the cream, then put his cookie on the saucer and handed it to Reyes. She gave everything the once over, smiled, then returned to her chair.

Wallace waited until Mrs Davey was seated again. 'Mr Davey,' she said, 'the fire at the Green Cheese Entertainment building was most likely arson. It's very possible that we are looking at a homicide, as well.'

Perhaps anticipating the next question, the next comment, Davey stopped in mid-motion of tapping his ash into the ashtray. He resumed sitting in an upright position, looked at Wallace and said nothing. It was his wife who spoke up.

'Homicide?'

'Murder, Mrs Davey,' Reyes said, helpfully, munching half of his cookie. 'There was a body in the fire.'

'Oh, my!' she said.

'We spoke with a Sonny Giordano...' said Wallace.

Davey sat back and took a drag. 'He's a liar.'

'Excuse me?'

'I don't even know what he said. It doesn't matter. It's a lie.'

'Giordano suggested that you were extremely angry about losing the bid and swore revenge.'

'That's what I'm saying. Sonny Giordano and his brother-in-law have no class.'

'You didn't threaten him?'

'No, sir. He's full of it. Was I frustrated? Sure. Pearl Construction has been getting a lot of jobs lately that...' He stopped and sipped his coffee. 'Well, let's say they've gotten more than we have.'

'So you're saying you didn't tell him that you'd "get him"?'

'Maybe I said that, but it's like telling someone you'll kill them when you're mad. It's a figure of speech, that's all. You wouldn't really kill them.'

Mrs Davey squirmed in her chair.

'In other words, Giordano is over-reacting?'

'Pearl Construction underbid me fair and square. That's the way we do things. You win some, you lose some. I already told you, we're doing fine. Plenty of work.'

'How do you feel about Mr Giordano personally? You like him?'

'I'm not his friend, if that's what you're asking, but I don't hold any grudges when it comes to business. You can't afford to.'

'So there is no reason for you to want to burn down one of his sites?'

'Ha! What a laugh. Unlike Pearl, my family name means something in this town. Something good. Do you honestly believe I would risk everything we've built over all these years because I lost one construction job? Not likely.' He ground out his cigarette. 'Besides, Sonny Giordano is hardly more than a hired hand – a manager. Bart Pearl is the owner. If I was going to have a grudge, don't you think it would be with him?'

'Excuse me. I have to use the little girl's room.' Mrs Davey rose and walked around the coffee table toward the hallway.

Reyes started to rise but Mrs Davey urged him not to. 'No, please keep your seat. I'm sorry.' She glanced at her husband, then hurried out of the room.

'She's a little nervous,' Davey said. 'You

75

don't need her in here anyway, do you?'

'No. We came to see you. Why is she nervous?' Wallace asked.

'You know, police in the living-room. It tends to unnerve some people.'

'It doesn't bother you though, right?'

'Not at all.' He smiled. 'What else would you like to know?'

'Actually,' Wallace said. 'I was wondering if you would care to discuss some of the other run-ins you've had with Pearl in the past.'

'Run-ins?'

'Word is that you two were more than rivals.'

'That hound won't hunt, Detective. Pearl and I are in competition in the business of construction, and that's all.'

'Can you account for your whereabouts yesterday?'

Davey scooted forward in his chair. 'I know what you two are thinking, but I didn't burn down that construction site. I was home all night last night.'

'Came here straight from work did you? No stops?'

'No stops. Right home.'

'How long did it take you to get here from your office?'

'I'd say under twenty minutes last night.'

'And you left work at what, five?'

'Yes. Right around five.'

'The fire began sometime between five and

eight, Mr Davey.'

Davey tensed. He clenched his teeth, a streak of red flashed from his temple through his cheeks. 'It appears to me like you've made up your mind about some things and the implications are sounding pretty nasty. I don't like it. No sir, not one bit.'

Wallace followed. 'We're not accusing you of anything, Mr Davey. Since your name came up though, we do have to get a few details of your whereabouts. It's standard procedure, nothing more.'

'Is there anything else you need?'

'I thought you said your wife was the nervous one.'

'I've been accused of a lot of things in my life, but murder has never made the list. Or arson. It's a bit unsettling.'

'Let's try to wrap this up calmly. You were home last night, you said. What time did you get here?'

Davey opened his pack of cigarettes again, took one out and lit it. 'Detective, I'm not comfortable answering any more questions. Really. I think I had better call my attorney before I say anything else.'

'If you think that's necessary, it certainly is one of the options open to you.'

'What are the other ones?'

'If you have nothing to hide, answering our questions gets everything wrapped up and we can move on to the next person.'

'Uh-huh. Yeah. Well, I'm going to wait until my attorney is present and you can think what you want.'

'We can take this up at another time, then.' Wallace put her notebook into her pocket. 'Thanks for your time.' She turned to Reyes. 'Partner, we're heading out. Mr Davey has declined further comment.'

Reyes walked straight to the door.' He paused long enough to say, 'Thank your wife for the coffee.'

'I will.'

The detectives stepped outside. Davey closed the door. Wallace and Reyes climbed into the car. 'What's up? You got something?' Reyes asked.

'I'm not sure. Both of them were nervous but they seemed willing to answer our questions up to a point.'

'I think it was when you suggested murder and arson.'

'That did kind of put a damper on things, didn't it?'

A red Cadillac CTS backed down the Daveys' driveway.

'Check it out,' Reyes said. 'It's the wife.'

'I wonder where she's going?'

'What d'ya think? Should we follow her?'

'Nah, let her go.'

The dispatcher's voice belched from the radio, a call to 'all units'. Wallace paused midway through opening the door. 'Let's see what this is first.'

'All units. Be on the lookout for Bartholomew Pearl. White male. Five foot ten inches. One hundred sixty pounds. Pearl failed to report for a standard parole meeting with the DA.'

The report went on, giving Pearl's home address on North Formosa and the business address of Pearl Construction on North La Jolla in West Hollywood.

'Well, now, what the hell do you think that's about? I thought he was in jail.'

'And now he's missing.'

Reyes got on the radio to Brooks.

'What can I do for you, Sal?'

'Any luck on the ID of our John Doe?'

Brooks chuckled.

'You're kidding, right? Hackett's probably not outa bed yet.'

'Well, tell him he could save time. Have him compare with the records of one Bartholomew Pearl, recently inside.'

Brooks didn't reply. Wallace gave Reyes a quizzical expression.

'Sarge, you still there?'

'Yeah, I'm here, Sal. You said Bart Pearl, right?'

'Yep. That name mean something to you?'

'You could say that. He's the low-life who shot Cresner.'

'And he's out?'

'He shouldn't be.'

Wallace tapped Reyes on the shoulder and pointed toward the garage, where Samuel Davey was backing out of the driveway in a dark blue Continental. Reyes drew his hand across his throat and Wallace walked over to the bottom of the driveway, her hand on her gun.

'Hold it, Mr Davey,' she shouted, then rapped on the rear windshield. The car juddered to a halt, and the side window hummed down.

From his position, Reyes could see Davey thump the steering column as Wallace motioned for him to get out. It was a long-shot, but the only one they had.

8

Reyes led Davey into Interview Room One, while Wallace held open the door. 'Have a seat, Mr Davey. We'll be right with you.'

Davey hitched his pants up and reached into his pockets, probably for the cigarettes they'd already taken off him, along with his wallet, keys and loose change. 'We could have done this at my house. You didn't have to drag me down here.'

'Uh-huh. I seem to remember you saying you didn't want to talk at your house.'

'Can I smoke?'

'Of course you can't smoke,' said Reyes.

He closed the door and followed Wallace down the hall to the break room. The coffee pot had a small glob of brown liquid at the bottom that resembled crude oil. Wallace dumped the brew in the sink and started a fresh pot. An approximate dental comparison, featuring a distinctive chip to the upper left lateral, had all but confirmed yesterday's corpse as that of Bartholomew Pearl.

'You don't think he killed Pearl, do you?' Reyes said. He slid a dollar into the Coke machine and pushed the button. The dispenser sounded like a bowling alley as it ejected the can and change. 'That's what you're thinking, isn't it?'

'If I told you what I'm thinking, you'd think that I was crazy.'

'Try me.'

'It's almost as though Davey is guilty, but I think someone is trying to frame him.'

'Shall we go see what we can find out?'

'It'll do his soul good to sweat a bit. Has he asked for his attorney?'

'Funny, as soon as his wife was out of the way, he went quiet about that.'

Brooks walked into the coffee room with the look of a gargoyle – gray, stone-faced. 'Is there any coffee?'

'Almost ready,' Wallace said. 'Are you okay?'

Brooks slid his cup down the counter and took a seat at the small table. 'It doesn't make sense. Pearl was supposed to be in jail, awaiting trial. How the hell did he get out?'

'Damned if I know,' Wallace said. 'I'll bet he wishes he hadn't.'

'Looks like justice might have been served, though.' Reyes took a gulp of Coke.

'Justice? Hardly,' Brooks said. 'I've called the Los Angeles Police Protective League. They said they would issue a statement denouncing his release. You saw Jerry last night. He looked damn awful. How can they let the guy who was responsible for that walk?'

'Actually, Phil and I left before Cresner showed. He looked bad did he?'

'That's an understatement. Maybe it's the Marine in him, but any other guy would still be in bed. Not Jerry, though. No. He's up and trying to return to the fight, but he had to have been in a lot of pain. Jesus, I wish you had seen him.'

Wallace poured two cups of coffee and handed one to Brooks.

'Thanks. Yeah. I swear, I'm going to find out. Somebody either screwed up or some sleazy judge got paid his pound of flesh.'

'You think a judge might be on the take?' Reyes considered that possibility. A crooked judge was almost as bad as finding out your mama was a hooker. It happened, of course, but he sure hoped it wasn't true now.

'Can you think of any other way Pearl got out while waiting trial on attempted murder?'

'Maybe some lawyer found a loophole,' Reyes said. 'It wouldn't be the first time.'

'I'm going to rectify the situation,' Brooks said.

Wallace blew on her coffee and took a sip. 'Tread lightly.'

'What's that supposed to mean?'

'The DA's office would have to have authorized the release. You should proceed with caution.'

Brooks clutched his mug. 'I'm nearing my Thirty – I haven't got anything to worry about.'

'Yeah, but we have. All I'm saying is, you're a detective. Nose around a little bit.'

Silence filled the room.

'Yeah, you're right, of course.' He placed the mug on the table. 'A thousand more cups until retirement.' Brooks rose and walked out.

Wallace turned to Reyes. 'Let's go see a man about a murder.'

Reyes led the way back to the IR.

'Well, it's about damned time,' Davey said.

'How about you hear us out first? Maybe we can save a lot of time and trouble. We only have a few things we have to get cleared up.' Reyes took a seat across from Davey.

Davey sighed. 'Okay. Okay. But if it sounds

like you're trying to railroad me, I'm asking for my lawyer.'

'Fair enough. Let's get started. Our investigators determined that the fire was intentionally set, and it looks fairly likely that Mr Crispy once went by the name of Bartholomew Pearl.'

'I don't care if they determined that men from Mars had a weenie roast. It has nothing to do with me. And I had nothing to do with Pearl's death. He was always a little red in the face. Maybe he ... what do you call it ... spontaneously combusted.'

Reyes sniggered.

'This isn't a joke, Mr Davey,' said Wallace. 'Ignore my partner.'

Davey gave her a bored look and waved his hand.

'My condolences to anyone who gave a shit about that low-life.'

The cuss word sounded strange coming from Davey's mouth. With his wife away from his side, he was a bit cockier.

'Mr Davey,' continued Wallace, 'we have a body and a motive.'

'Well, you ain't got me. You think I'm the only guy in the world that has ever had an argument with that son of a bitch?'

'Do you want to tell us what happened?'

'This is insane. It's beyond insane.' His eyes rolled to the ceiling, then focused on Wallace. He set his jaw, clasped his hands in front of

84

him, resting them on the table. 'Look, detectives, I keep saying this over and over again. I had nothing to do with this. I didn't set the fire. I didn't kill Pearl. I heard he was in jail. Couldn't happen to a nicer guy.'

'When was the last time you saw Bartholomew Pearl?' Wallace asked.

'I don't know. Sometime before he was arrested.'

'Your wife said you were home all night.'

'I told you that I was.'

'We checked with your secretary,' he looked at the notebook again. 'Miss Bridget McGuire?'

'And what did Bridget have to say?'

'She said she was sure you were there except...'

Davey let out a huge sigh. 'Spit it out, detective.'

'She ran some errands for the company. She was gone yesterday from about one-thirty until four.'

'So what? She runs errands all the time.'

'The fire could have been started during the time she was out.'

'You think she set the fire?' said Davey, a smirk creeping across his face. 'God knows if she was running errands or burning down buildings. If you see her, let her know that if she was out killing people on company time, I'm docking her pay.'

Reyes leaned back. 'You think this is a

joke?' he asked. 'What it means is that Miss McGuire is unable to provide you with an alibi.'

'No, I don't think this is a joke,' Davey said.

'Wait a minute.' Reyes turned slightly and froze. 'Listen.'

Though muffled, the sound of shouting came from somewhere in the station – close to the interview room. Wallace tensed. 'Sit right there, Mr Davey.'

Reyes stood 'Let me take a look.'

'Hey,' Davey said, rising from his seat. 'That sounds like my wife.'

'Stay put.' Reyes held up his hand.

'It's bad enough you dragged me down here. I don't want you nailing my wife as well.'

'You're not giving orders here, Davey.' Wallace moved toward him. 'Sit!'

'I'll look.' Reyes pulled open the door. Mrs Davey was screaming at Brooks and Captain Siley at the top of her lungs.

'...so how the heck could he have been somewhere else? You can't be in two places at one time. Not even the great Sam Davey can pull that one off. My God, he was sitting in his living-room watching *Deal or No Deal*.'

'Mrs Davey, we are simply asking your husband some questions...'

'Oh, sure. My husband is an honest man, trying to earn an honest living.'

Davey ploughed past Wallace. Reyes moved to stop him, but Wallace shook her head. Davey trotted the fifteen feet to where his wife stood. 'Janet. It's okay. Everything's okay.'

'It's not right, Sam. You jump through all their hoops, you...'

'Shut up, Janet!' Davey said.

He hugged her and looked at Brooks, then the other three officers. 'Could I have a minute, please? Then we can finish up in there.'

Wallace nodded yes. 'Go ahead.' She looked at Siley and Brooks. 'We've got it.'

'That's good enough for me,' said Siley.

Brooks hesitated. 'Do you think he had something to do with it?'

Wallace checked over her shoulder. Davey and his wife had walked into the hallway outside the Pit, far enough away that they couldn't be overheard. 'Honestly,' Wallace said, 'I'm not sure.'

'He comes across as a solid enough citizen, but I'm not buying it,' Reyes said. 'I don't know that he killed Pearl, but I don't think he's as innocent as he appears.'

Davey returned to the group. Reyes gestured for him to enter the interview room, as Siley showed Mrs Davey down the hall, toward the front door.

Back in IR One, the three sat quietly for a second or two.

'Thanks,' Davey said. 'You know, for

letting me talk with Janet. She's a little high strung sometimes. She was trying to protect me, but she knows nothing about how the business works.'

'So what was that she was saying about you jumping through hoops?' asked Reyes.

'It was nothing. She just sees all the forms from the City, y'know, procedural stuff Licenses, registrations, inspections, standard bullshit...'

He's hiding something, thought Reyes. He silenced his wife quickly, like he was scared she was going to say too much.

'You weren't having any problems with the business other than paperwork?'

'That's it. Like I said, she doesn't understand. I'd come home bitching about the paperwork and she took it wrong. That's part of the reason I moved into film builds. Less restrictions.'

'All right,' said Reyes. 'Would you care to submit to a gunshot residue test?'

'What's that, Detective?'

'It will ascertain if you've fired a weapon in the last forty-eight hours.'

'Sure, of course. Anything to help.'

'Great, you hang tight for a minute,' said Reyes. 'My partner and I have to consult on a few things.'

Davey folded his hands in front of him. 'If you're going to be a long time, how about I go outside and have a smoke?'

'Sit tight,' Reyes said. They stepped from the room and closed the door, leaving Davey alone with his thoughts.

'I want to hold him for a bit yet,' Reyes said.

'Really? Why?'

'I think there's something he's keeping from us. I'd like a bit more time to figure out what.'

'The GSR won't be worth shit. He's a heavy smoker, he's changed his clothes, washed.'

'I just wanted to rattle him some more.'

Siley came back into the corridor. 'Talk to El Capitano,' she said.

'The wife's pretty angry,' he said, 'but I calmed her down.'

'Must be all the practice with Mrs Siley,' joked Wallace.

'You got that right.'

'Captain,' Reyes said. 'Do you have a problem with us holding Davey? I want to check him out a little more.'

'You charging him?'

'No. But I think if we hold him in connection he might give up something. I'd like to give him a GSR.'

Siley looked at Wallace, then back to Reyes. 'If the test comes back negative, cut him loose. If you need to, bring him back in.'

'Aw, come on Captain...'

'What's the point, Sal? He'll lawyer up and

then it'll make things even harder in the long term.'

Reyes nodded. Siley was right. 'Whatever you say, boss.'

'Anyway,' said Siley. 'I have a hot one and no one else is available. Can you two handle it?'

'What about Kahn and Wagner?' Wallace asked.

Siley shook his head. 'You didn't hear? They've busted some juvenile's arm.'

'Harlen's a liability,' said Reyes.

'This was Don, as a matter of fact,' said the Captain.

'Well, you can bet Wagner was involved somehow,' said Wallace, rolling her eyes. 'Joanna and Emilio?'

'Wrapping up a drug-store stabbing.'

'Looks like it's ours, then,' Reyes said. 'What's the headline?'

'There's been a shooting at the Council offices.'

'At the City Council?' Wallace asked.

'I'm afraid so. This one is going to be front page grist, so be ready.'

'Great. Do you have an ID on the victim?'

'His name is Theodore Simons. He's one of the council members.'

9

The City Council building on North Spring Street was already surrounded by press vans. 'Damn, these guys don't miss a trick,' said Wallace.

They parked as near the door as possible and found the lobby jammed with people, half trying to get out, the other half, mostly media, trying to get in.

'God, what a madhouse,' said Reyes. Wallace could tell he was still a little pissed about the call they'd just received from the sergeant. The GSR on Davey had come back negative.

The officers who had responded to the call had reinforced the security staff and were carefully limiting access to everyone but staff and police. Wallace and Reyes squeezed forward until they reached the metal scanner – the sole entry point.

'Detective Wallace? Jimmy Dunn, *Hollywood News*. Can you tell us anything?' The reporter jammed a microphone in her face.

'You can have my "no comment" comment now,' Wallace said. 'Or you can wait until later.'

Another voice from behind him in the

mob of microphones and recording devices shouted: 'Do you have any information yet as to what caused Councilor Simons to kill himself?'

Wallace spoke fast. 'Folks, right now, I know nothing. I'm on my way up. Hopefully, the next time you see me, I'll know something. Thank you.'

'Oh, come on,' the new *Times* beat reporter Terri Snowden called out. 'You have to know something, Officer.'

'Ask around. You'll find that's not the case,' Wallace replied, and slipped through the scanner, setting off lights and buzzers. They flashed and buzzed again as Reyes followed quickly behind.

'Fourth floor,' a uniformed officer by the elevator told them.

'Thanks.' Wallace stepped inside and pushed the button for the fourth floor. The doors closed, shutting out the chaos in the lobby.

'I know they have to report the news but damn, can't they be more civilized about it?'

'You're getting pretty good at dodging questions,' said Reyes.

'I've learned to give them double-talk. By the time they figure out that I didn't say anything, I'm usually behind the yellow line.'

The doors opened on the fourth floor and an atmosphere like a wake. A dozen people stood in worried groups of two or three in the hall outside the council offices. Two women holding tissues leant close together, one with mascara smudged under her eyes.

A uniformed officer directed them toward the council office.

Inside, more small groups of staff members milled around in the reception area and down the hallways. Their whispered conversations halted as the detectives passed. Officers who had responded to the nine-one-one call stood near the door to Simons' office.

Wallace recognized an old friend, De-Marcus Mason. 'DeMarcus, how are you, my man?'

'Hey, Phil. Pretty good. You guys going to handle this one?'

'Yeah. You in charge?'

'More or less.' He turned and looked down the hall. 'The ADA is here. I have no idea why. She's over with the other council members. Away from the riff-raff and staff.'

'You know my partner, Sal Reyes?'

'Hi, Sal.'

Reyes nodded.

'I know you don't like to waste time, Phil, so let me get right to it. It appears that Theodore Simons, a city council member involved with construction, shot himself in the right temple sometime this morning, although no one heard the shot.'

'Maybe he used a silencer?' Reyes said. 'Or

93

someone else did.'

'Not likely. The gun is lying on the floor. No silencer.'

'Keep an open mind,' Wallace said. 'You never know.'

'Good luck with that theory,' Mason said. 'We don't have an official guess on the time of death as yet, but based on some initial interviews, we think he got in early, which is not unusual by the way, and was dead some time before noon. His secretary, Muriel Parks, discovered the body a few minutes before twelve, when she checked to see if he wanted her to get him anything for lunch. The supporting cast should be here any second.'

Behind him, Wallace saw Barclay-Jones at one end of the hall.

'The ADA's following us around today, Sal.'

'We'd better look busy,' he replied. 'De-Marcus, are all these other people staff?'

Mason gestured to a uniformed officer. 'Sampson, verify that we have everyone ID'd. If they don't belong on this floor, get them into a side office, and let me know.'

'Will do,' she said.

'You really think it's not suicide?' Mason asked.

'I don't know,' said Reyes, 'but if it isn't, I don't want someone slipping out of here without us knowing who the hell they are and why they're here.'

'Point taken,' Mason said. 'Of course, there was plenty of time for a killer to have escaped before we got here. But, better safe than sorry. We'll check out the folks down the hall. Oh, and when you're ready, Simons' secretary is down the hall in the other direction.' He pointed. 'She's pretty shaken up.'

'Can we talk with her?'

'Sure, follow me.'

Mason led them toward the two women holding tissues. He addressed the one wearing a lilac skirt and maroon blouse.

'Mrs Parks, these are Detectives Wallace and Reyes. They're investigating Mr Simons' suicide.'

Muriel Parks nodded meekly, and muttered something to the younger lady beside her, who squeezed her hand and walked away. 'I'll help in any way I can, detectives.'

'Perhaps you can tell us what alerted you to Mr Simons' office,' said Wallace. 'Had he seemed all right earlier this morning?'

'I'm afraid I couldn't tell you,' said Mrs Parks. 'You see, I only came in just before twelve. Theo ... Mr Simons ... had told me I could take the morning off.'

'I see,' said Wallace. 'Is that usual?'

'Mr Simons is a very considerate employer, detective,' said Mrs Parks, dabbing at her eyes, 'but he doesn't often suggest such an arrangement, no.'

'Do you know if he was meeting someone this morning?'

'I'd have to check his calendar. Mr Simons is ... was...' Tears began to flow again. 'I'm sorry,' she mumbled. 'Mr Simons was a busy man.'

'I understand, Mrs Parks, and thank you for your help. If we could see that calendar, I'd be very grateful.'

'Of course.' Muriel Parks turned and walked away.

Wallace turned back to Mason. 'I think we'll go peek in on the vic.'

Wallace pushed on the partially-closed office door. She and Reyes stepped in and closed the door behind them. The air-con hummed, but the smell of blood was still in the air. Theodore Simons sat slumped down and obviously very dead in his chair. His head was cocked to the right side and slightly forward. He had bled profusely all over the right shoulder of his jacket and his shirt front.

Wallace walked around the desk and stood next to the dead man. Reyes joined her on the other side. Wallace reached in her pocket, took out a pair of latex gloves and pulled them on. She squatted down in order to get a look at the wound.

'Hmm. There appears to be a single entrance wound. Accurate, too. I'd guess the gun was a couple of inches from the temple at most.'

The gun was lying on the floor, right where he would have dropped it if he'd shot himself

'How is it that not one person heard anything?' said Reyes.

Wallace inserted a pencil into the barrel of the gun that lay on the floor, directly below the dead man's right hand. She stood back up and examined it. 'I'm not sure.' She stared at the markings on the dull-gray barrel of the semi-automatic. She read: *Made in Russia by IMEZ.*

The door opened and Sean Nazer from Forensics came into the office. 'Got room for one more?'

'Your timing couldn't be better,' said Wallace. 'You boys are familiar with all sorts of weapons. Do you know what kind of gun this is?'

Nazer walked over, took one look and said, 'That's a Makarov PM. Russian.'

'Ah. So that's what *Made in Russia* means. We don't see many of these around here.'

'Nope. A while back Narcotics busted up a Russian gang operating down near the harbor area. Smuggling mostly. They had a butt-load of these, but we must have missed a previous shipment. They're becoming more common on the streets, especially further east.'

'I wonder how our boy Simons got one?'

Reyes asked.

Wallace experienced a vague feeling of unease thinking back to her conversation with David. Guns. This couldn't be connected, could it?

'They pop up now and then. For a councilman to have one is kind of strange, though. The few I've run across have been taken from the cold, dead hand of some Hispanic gang member.'

'You come alone or is everybody here?' Wallace asked.

'Alone. I imagine the others will be here in a minute. Checking out the reported suicide of a city official usually brings out the A-team.' He picked up a photograph from the councilman's desk. 'Nice looking kids.' He placed it back on the desk and looked at Wallace. 'You done or do you want me to wait?'

'Give us a few more minutes.'

'I have a bullet hole over here in the wall,' Reyes said. He pointed at a small hole about six inches to the left of a Cézanne print that hung over the credenza. There was another pale space on the wall beside it, where a picture had once hung for some time.

The middle drawer of the desk was blocked by Simons' corpse. Wallace opted to wait for the forensics crew before moving the body and turned instead to the top right-hand drawer. 'Oh. What have we here?'

'Find something interesting?' Reyes asked.

Wallace pulled out the pistol from the drawer. Its ivory handles were beautifully polished. 'Now, this one I recognize,' she said. 'It's a good old American Colt .45 Peacemaker.'

'Son of a bitch,' Nazer said. 'Now that's a gun. You would think that if he killed himself, this is the one he would have used. It would have guaranteed that he did the job right.'

Wallace laid the gun on the desk-top, checked the rest of the drawer, and then opened the large bottom drawer. She removed a wooden box and read the inscription on the brass plate fixed to the top. *Captain Theodore Simons. A Troop, 1st Squadron, 4th US. Cavalry, DOU6, Desert Storm.*

Wallace opened the box and ran her finger over the red velvet liner.

'Maybe that's why he didn't use it,' Reyes said. 'It was special. A souvenir.'

'Then you have to ask yourself a question. If it was that special, why wasn't it in the box? Why was it lying unprotected in the top drawer?'

'Maybe for protection,' Reyes said. He was rummaging through some files.

'That's what I was thinking, but...'

'But what?' Nazer asked.

'What does a man who is about to kill himself need protection from?' Wallace laid the box aside and reached into the drawer. 'Here's a good companion to a loaded weapon.' She pulled out an almost empty bottle of Vat 69 Scotch, and two tubs of pills.

'He seems to have had a lot of issues,' said Reyes.

Wallace finished checking the drawer and turned her focus to the desk-top. There was an eight by ten photo of a red-haired woman – his wife most likely – in a silver filigree frame. On the back was a gold sticker on which was stamped Al-Jahiz and some Arabic looking scribble below that. The second photo, the one Nazer had looked at, was in a smaller but similar frame. A blond boy and a red-headed girl. Both kids dressed to the nines. The little girl looked about seven, the boy no more than ten.

You're the man of the house, now, thought Wallace.

The last photo was in a black plastic frame with the words *Disney Cruise* embossed across the bottom. Simons, his wife, two kids and two older people. Maybe his parents, or hers. The group was standing together by a railing, all grinning.

Wallace spun the desk-top calendar to take a look at his appointments for the day. Something skittered across the desk, Reyes caught it, then held it up.

'Found the shell casing.' He unzipped an evidence bag, and placed it inside.

Wallace returned to the councilman's schedule.

7.00: Duke
14.30: Jackson Pilar
15.45: Antonio and Maria Mendez
17.00: Call Rev. Turner
19.00: Dinner at Le Cochon qui Vole. Confirm!

There were three Post-It notes stuck to a writing tablet. Wallace picked up the notes. The top one said: *Mr Lambeau @ Le Cochon qui Vole wants you to confirm dinner reservations for tonight.*

'Hey Sal,' said Wallace. 'Why make a note to confirm your dinner reservations if you were going to kill yourself?'

'Beats me,' said Reyes. He was going through a filing cabinet on the other side of the room.

The second phone message: 'Dwayne called. He has an opening first thing. Do you want it?'

Dwayne? Dwayne Duke? A breakfast meeting maybe.

Wallace noted the name. She'd speak to Muriel again later.

Reyes walked to the desk and laid several folders on the corner. 'Too many folders to go through now. We'll probably need to box 'em and bring 'em downtown. However, I did pull out these.'

'Anything of interest?'

'Pearl Construction and Sphinx Construction.'

'No shit. And?'

'Well, if the paperwork is anything to go by, I'd say Pearl was the bigger outfit. It looks like they bid on a hell of a lot more projects than Davey. They also got a lot more. Pearl has three folders. Most of the others have one, including Sphinx.' He flicked through one of the files. 'In fact, Davey's work seems to have pretty much dried up about six months ago.'

'Maybe it's all the *forms*,' said Wallace.

'You weren't buying that either, eh?' Reyes went back to the cabinet and looked again. 'If Davey's family has been in the business as long as he says, I would have thought they were fairly used to paperwork.'

'There won't be records here for the studio builds, of course. Those don't pass through the City, except for the license.'

Wallace eyed the files. 'Why don't you see if you can find jobs where they bid against one another? Check out Phase One of the Green Cheese job.'

'We need to take his computer. It would make this a lot easier.'

A strident voice from the hallway penetrated the office. 'Move aside, officers.'

Wallace glanced at Reyes. 'What the...?' She walked to the door. 'What in the hell is going on out here?'

A tall, thin, red-haired man with wire-rimmed glasses and a badge clipped to his jacket pocket stepped up to her – too close.

Wallace put her hand on the man's chest.

'Hold it right there. Who the hell do you think you are, barging into my crime scene like this?'

The man pulled out his identification. 'Riley O'Conner, FID. And *your* crime scene is now *our* crime scene. We're taking over this case.'

'O'Conner. Aren't you part of David Wallace's team?'

'Yes. And yes, I know who you are, Detective.'

'Where's David?'

'Not with us right now. You have your orders. Vacate the scene.'

'I don't take orders from you, Red. You got something in writing? If not, I'll call in before surrendering the site to you and your ... squad.'

'Be my guest.'

Wallace eyed the FID team, all suited and hovering behind their asshole of a boss like a gang behind the schoolyard bully. She pulled out her cell phone and hit two, the auto-dial for the station. The phone rang twice.

'Wagner. Hollywood.'

'Wagner? Where's Brooks or Captain Siley?'

'Shit. They're ... er...'

'Come on, man. I've got a problem here. FID is claiming they have orders to take over the investigation. I have to know where this is coming from and I need to know now.'

'Phil. Your husband is here.'

David was at the Precinct? This had to be connected with the guns.

'Is he looking for me?' she asked, hopeful still that there was an innocent explanation for all this.

'No. He and his FID boys came in, talked to Siley for a minute or two and then took Brooks into IR One.'

10

Wallace lunged from the car. She slammed the door and stormed over to Wagner and Kahn, who stood in the shade of a ginkgo tree. 'What in the hell is going on?'

'We figured if anybody knew, it'd be you,' Wagner said.

'Me? Why would I know? Some FID prick threw me off my own crime scene not thirty minutes ago.'

'Yeah, well, it's your worse-half leading the inquisition in there.' Wagner threw his cigarette down and stomped on it. 'We thought maybe you knew this was coming so you made sure you weren't around.'

'You dumb...' Wallace said. 'Look, the only reason I wasn't here is because Sal and I had to cover while you two explained why you messed up some kid during an arrest. Otherwise, you would have been over there and we would have been here.'

'Bullshit,' Wagner said. 'You trying to tell me your husband didn't clue you in about whatever the fuck is going down in there?'

He had a point, but Wallace wasn't in the mood to tussle with Wagner today. 'Have you ever dealt with FID?' she said. 'They're so tight-lipped they wouldn't tell their mommas if they shit in their pants as a baby. David and I don't lie in bed at night and make pillow-talk about internal affairs. I'm as clueless as you are.'

'No one's as clueless as Harlen...' said Kahn, then looked hurt when no one smiled.

Wallace headed toward the door. Reyes followed behind.

I'm going to kill David. He didn't want me getting caught flat-footed. Ha!

Wallace stormed past the locker room, turned left down the center aisle of the Pit. Coombs and Albanese were deep in conversation.

'Joanne, what in the hell is happening?'

Coombs spun in her chair. 'Don't ask me. I don't know anything. FID still has Brooks in Room One. He hasn't called his Union Rep. Siley's been in his office with the door shut. FID agents are running around here like cockroaches ... sorry, Phil. No offense.'

'Is this something to do with the City Council case?' asked Reyes.

Coombs shrugged and Wallace saw the door to IR One open.

A white male, over six foot tall, short black hair, stepped out first, followed by Brooks and then another man, who was a carbon-copy of the first man except he was black. Brooks was staring at the floor, silent. He looked tired, but there appeared a familiar grim resolve in his expression.

Kahn jogged to the corner and peeked down the hall. A moment later, he returned to the huddle of detectives. 'They all went into Siley's office.'

Before anyone could speak, Wallace's husband came down the hall, followed by Jerry Cresner hobbling, leaning heavy on his cane. He was accompanied by a female FID officer with bobbed brunette hair. She was shorter than her male counterparts, but otherwise cut from the same mold.

'Mother-fuck,' Wagner said. 'Now what? Why is Cresner here? He's not Homicide.'

'This is getting damned strange,' Albanese said.

Wallace's heart was sinking. David must have made some kind of mistake.

'Well, I've had enough.' Wagner raced over and blocked the way to the interview rooms. David stopped and looked at him as though he was a lab specimen. Wagner sure did look a mess.

'Okay, that's about enough of this bull-shit,' Wagner said. 'You need to tell us what the hell you're up to. Why are you dragging cops into interrogation?'

'Step aside, officer,' David said. 'You don't want a part of me.'

'Screw you. We're not some drug cartel, we're your fellow officers. We deserve respect.'

'I'm going to say it once more. Step aside.' Wallace had to admire the way he took no crap. She guessed it was a daily occurrence.

Wagner didn't move, but Kahn stepped forward, and placed his arm around Wagner's chest. 'Come on, Harlen, let 'em do their job.'

'This fucking stinks,' said Wagner.

'You can't afford another strike, partner.'

Wagner took a step back.

'I appreciate your concern for your fellow officers,' David said, 'but I'm not at liberty to discuss the current situation. I can tell you that we simply need to ask a few questions of these men.' The FID group went into the interview room, with Cresner leading the way.

'Now what?' Wagner said. His anger was gone, replaced by an exasperated tone. 'Are we going to just sit around and do nothing?'

Coombs walked by and quietly slipped into the Observation Room. *Smart cookie*, thought Wallace. She and the others quickly followed.

It was small, designed for use by three or four people, but now all six detectives squeezed in.

Coombs powered up the recording equipment. The video screen illuminated, but remained snow-filled gray. 'Damn. They must have switched off the link.'

'How about audio?' Albanese asked.

Coombs adjusted the volume and to Wallace's surprise, they could clearly hear the conversation in IR One.

Wallace tensed as the voice of her husband crackled through the speakers.

'We need to know where you were this morning until noon.'

Reyes gave her a look. Surely they didn't think Cresner had something to do with Simons' death?

'Looks like they flipped only one of the switches,' Coombs said. 'Thank God for the technologically-challenged.'

'Shush,' said Wallace.

'I was at home,' Cresner said.

'With your wife?'

'She left around seven for work.'

'According to your file, your authorization to return to work form states that you are able to drive. Is that form wrong?'

'No. I can drive.'

'And did you drive anywhere this morning?'

'My car is in the shop. It wouldn't start so we had the guy at our local garage come tow it in.

Maybe it was because it was sitting around for three months while I recuperated from being shot. I assume you all remember that?'

'Sure we do, Jerry. *Before we get to that, why don't you go ahead and finish telling us about the rest of your morning.'*

'There is no rest. A friend brought me to work around ten. I worked. Your people picked me up.'

The OR was suddenly silent. Coombs instantly began fiddling with the buttons. 'It's all working,' she whispered. 'I don't think anyone's talking in the other room.'

A few more seconds passed. David finally said, '*And?'*

'That's it, unless you want me to list my trips to the bathroom.'

'You weren't at your desk when we came to pick you up.'

'I was in the break room eating lunch. Mary packed me a cold meat-loaf sandwich. You guys picked me up at lunch-time for Christ's sake.'

'I don't get it,' Wallace said. 'Are they suggesting he had something to do with Simons' death?'

'Oh-oh' Coombs said. 'I think ... shh! Somebody left the room. Everybody quiet.'

The detectives froze. Wallace heard a female voice right outside the door. Wagner leaned his ear against it. No one moved, except for Coombs, who slid her hand to the volume control panel and hit *Mute*.

Wagner turned around. 'I think she went

back in,' he whispered. 'She called somebody and told them to check out Cresner's story.'

'They don't believe him,' Coombs said. She turned the volume back up.

'*...and you don't know anything about the death of council member Simons. Is that what you're saying?*'

'*I heard that it was a suicide.*'

'*Please answer the question. Did you have anything to do with council member Simons' death?*'

'*No. Is that clear enough?*'

'*Let's try another one, then. Did you know Bartholomew Pearl?*'

Silence filled both rooms. Coombs once again checked the volume controls in the OR and shrugged. 'We're okay.'

'I don't like the fact that he didn't answer right away,' Kahn said.

'Me, neither.' Coombs turned to the other detectives. 'He sounds nervous. If he was my suspect...'

Wallace held up a hand. 'Let's not go there.'

'*Can't think of an answer to that one, Jerry?*' Agent Wallace asked. '*It's a simple yes or no. Did you know Bart Pearl?*'

'*No. I didn't know him. I ... I sometimes have trouble remembering exactly what happened, is all. I've been over this before.*'

'*Humor me, go over it again,*' David said.

Wallace heard Cresner give a deep sigh.

'*There was this alley. Some guy was arguing with Pearl. Of course, at the time I didn't know that's who it was. I was off-duty, but it looked to me like the situation was turning ugly. These two guys were sort of dancing, like. You know? They had a hold of each other and were moving farther down the alley – push, shove, push, shove – that kind of thing.'*

'And being a conscientious cop, you decided to, shall we say, cut in?'

'I thought it was my duty to stop them before things took a turn for the worse.'

'Go on.' Another FID agent had spoken.

'I was only a couple of feet away when I identified myself as a cop. Without saying a word, Pearl pulled a gun. I grabbed his hand, the one with the gun in it, and pushed down. He squeezed the trigger. The bullet hit me right here.'

'And then?' a female voice asked.

'I tried to hold on but I was falling. He whipped me around and slammed me into the wall. It was like being hit by a train. I dropped hard on my ass. I thought I was going to pass out but I fought it. After a second or two I felt myself pitching to one side. That was it.'

'Were you able to see what Pearl did next, or what happened to the other man you claim was there?'

'I don't claim anything. He was there.'

'Did you notice what he did when the shooting started?' David asked.

'He started running when Pearl and I locked up. I was too busy to see where he went.'

'And Pearl? What happened to Pearl?'

'I don't know. I passed out.'

'Let's go back to the third man. It was a man, right? Not a woman?'

'I think it was a man.'

'You think it was, huh?' the female FID agent said. 'Not sure any more?'

'It happened kind of fast. I wasn't checking IDs or grabbing tits. You'll notice I haven't grabbed yours yet.'

'That's enough,' Wallace's husband said. 'Try to remember we're all cops here.'

'I will, if you will,' Cresner said.

'Can you describe this person who we'll call the third man?' David asked.

'Hispanic, I think. He and Pearl were about the same size.'

'And you're sure there was this third person?'

'Yes. How many times do I have to say it?'

'Until we get it right. We listened to your story. Now, see how ours sounds. You and Pearl met to discuss business. Business that couldn't be conducted in a normal setting, so you turned to an alley. Things did not go well. Pearl shot you. He went to jail. You recovered. For no good reason, Pearl was released and a couple of days later, killed. Now, we have to ask ourselves, who would like to see Mr Pearl killed?'

Again awkward silence filled both rooms.

Damn. Coombs was right. The long hesitations weren't a good sign. Wallace looked around the room and wondered if everyone was thinking the same thing.

112

Perhaps Cresner was just having trouble focusing. He'd been through a lot the last three months, physically and mentally. And David and the other agent weren't wearing kid gloves. They were showing no respect for the man's record, or for his weakened state.

When Cresner broke the silence, his voice was croaky.

'And what business would I have with Pearl?'

'Now we're getting somewhere, Jerry,' said David. *'What business, indeed?'*

He smells blood, thought Wallace.

'Tell us about guns, Jerry...'

The door opened suddenly, and Brooks' face registered surprise.

'What in the hell?' Then anger creased Brooks' brow. 'Wait a damn minute. Are you guys listening in on Cresner's examination? Did you listen in on my little interview as well?' He barged through and hit the power button. 'That's none of your damn business.'

'No one's told us anything,' Kahn said. 'We were concerned about you and your buddy in there.'

'It sounds like FID believes that he may have been involved in the killing of Pearl,' Coombs said.

'What the hell do you know about it?' Brooks said. 'Jerry Cresner has been a cop since before you were in diapers. The man has given his blood for this city. What gives you the right to criticize him or to suspect

113

him of doing anything wrong?'

'She was only repeating what she overheard,' Wagner said.

'Well, she shouldn't have been listening. None of you should.'

'Hold it, now,' Kahn said. 'There was some pretty curious shit going down in the other room.'

'I don't know. I think Brooks is right,' Reyes said. 'We overstepped our boundaries.'

'What?' Coombs said.

'I mean, he's right, none of us should have been listening. It's like listening in on a confessional.'

'Bullshit,' Wagner said. 'We have a right to know, especially if one of us has flipped.'

'That's just it,' Reyes threw his hands up. 'We don't know that for a fact.'

'I have to confess that what I heard didn't sound good for your friend,' Wallace said. 'I know you guys were partners but...'

Brooks glared at her. 'Jesus, Phil, of all people, I didn't think you would stoop this low. Think what you want. I know the man.'

Siley appeared in the open door way. 'Good Christ, what in the world is everybody doing in here? Your desks are out there.'

'They had to find out what Jerry was being raked over the coals for,' Brooks said.

Wagner eased his way between Siley and the doorjamb, but the captain got in the way.

'None of you may like what's going on, but

we've got to live with it. I've been ordered to provide FID office space for the duration of their investigation.'

A collective groan went through the room.

'Captain,' said Wallace. 'If the Simons death is linked with Pearl's murder, we need to be all over that scene.'

Siley held up both palms. 'There's nothing I can do, Phil. FID are running a tight ship on Simons – they won't let anything leak.'

'Then we're putting the case together with one hand tied behind our back.'

'So be it, but stay out of their way. I don't want this department being obstructive.'

'Do we get to know what the hell it is that they're investigating?' Wagner asked.

'When it's the proper time, you'll be told. There are most likely going to be others called in for interviews. If you end up being one of those, cooperate. Pissing them off doesn't help anybody.'

'Fuck them.' Wagner tried to push past Siley.

'Goddamn it, Harlen. You'll do what I say or you'll be out of here. Now is not the time for bullshit.' Siley looked over the group. 'How about we start trying to solve a couple of murders instead of eavesdropping on a private matter?'

The phone rang. Wallace slipped out of the OR and hurried to the first desk she could reach. 'Hollywood Precinct, Detective

115

Wallace speaking.'

'Detective Wallace, this is Sergeant Evans, Wilshire. Are you working the Pearl case?'

'Amongst others,' she replied.

'We responded to a report of a break-in up on Lemon Grove. The place is registered to your vic. My guys are there now; wanna take a look?'

'Sure,' said Wallace. 'Give me the details.'

As she scribbled down the address, Reyes leaned over her cubicle wall.

'That a lead?'

'Thanks, detective.' She put down the phone and turned to her partner. 'That was Wilshire on the phone. Pearl's apartment has been broken into.'

Reyes grabbed his bottle of water. 'You going to tell FID?'

'Cooperate, my ass. Once they start scratching our back, I'll think about returning the favor. For now, let's keep it to ourselves.'

11

Wallace drove them in silence south along Northwestern toward Pearl's apartment. They stopped for a red light at the corner of Northwestern and Virginia, and Reyes stared out of the window at a sign on an empty lot. *Future Home of O'Hisser's Sports Bar and Grill. Gilcrest Construction.*

'I had a feeling Pearl and Simons were linked. Two deaths in twenty-four hours – same gun I bet. Simons takes out Pearl, then does himself.'

'And why would the good councilman shoot a successful building contractor, Sherlock?'

'Because Pearl had something on him.'

'And why'd he kill himself?'

'Oh, I don't know, Phil. Murderers aren't always logical. He got his revenge then couldn't live with himself, I guess.'

'Mm,' said Wallace, in a tone that suggested she thought Reyes' detective skills didn't amount to much.

Reyes reached into his rear pocket and pulled out a wad of papers he had jammed in there earlier. He had forgotten all about them until now. Reyes unfolded the sheets and smoothed them on the dashboard.

'What's that?' Wallace asked.

'When I was going through the contract folders at Simons' office, I found what I guess would be called the master list. It didn't have anything but the project name, the project number, the list of contractors who were bidding on it and who was awarded the deal. I had started checking things out when FID came a knocking.' He

117

smiled. 'I figured I had better grab what I could.'

'I'm impressed. What does it say?'

'Let me see.' Reyes checked the spread-sheet. 'Hell, these pages go back, what, about five years...' He ran his finger down the columns, flipped to the next pages and did the same. 'Okay.' He glanced over at Wallace. 'There are no details, of course, so there may be extenuating circumstances as to why someone was selected. All this spreadsheet does is list the final bid of each construction company and who the low bidder was. In the last five years where there was head to head competition, that is where both Davey and Pearl bid, it looks like Pearl took about seventy-five per cent of the jobs. I can see why Davey may have been getting frustrated. His bids were close every time but Pearl somehow managed to come in a per cent or two lower.'

'And? Perhaps Pearl was a better business-man. It's like Davey said, fair and square.'

'Or Pearl and Simons were in something together. You know, scratching each other's nuts.'

'I think you mean "backs".'

'Hey, I'm Latino. Lost in translation. So far, we don't have any link between Pearl and Simons that isn't purely circumstantial.'

'We would need to see the complete job files back in Simons' office, or check his bank details.'

'And, of course, we're not exactly on the A-list at that crime scene.'

Wallace dug in her jacket pocket, pulled out her notebook, and flipped it open on the center of the steering column. 'I meant to ask Simons' secretary – what was her name?'

'Parks.'

'Well, we need to talk to her again. Simons was due to meet someone called Duke this morning. I think the guy's first name might be Dwayne. Can you do a search?'

Reyes tapped the name into the car's computer, but the search came up blank. 'There's a Dukwon Duke and Dyana Dukes, but no Dwayne.'

'Figures.'

Wallace turned right on to Lemon Grove Avenue. The neighborhood had a little bit of this and a little bit of that. A dry cleaner, a limo company, a store-front psychic named Madame Geraldine, followed by gorgeous older homes, many apparently turned into condos or apartments.

They managed to find on-street parking two doors down from Pearl's apartment house. Reyes called in. 'This is Adam Six Nineteen. We're Code Six at Five-Five-Five-Three Lemon Grove.'

'Roger Adam Six Nineteen,' the dispatcher replied.

A white male, thirtyish, wearing a long-sleeve striped shirt and slacks stood with his arms folded in front of the building. He stared at the police car but didn't budge.

'It's nice to be wanted,' Reyes said, pulling the door handle and climbing out of the car.

'He doesn't look all that happy,' said Wallace.

The apartment building was on a bit of an incline, maybe ten or fifteen feet higher than the street. Concrete steps led to an elevated sidewalk, which continued to the stairs that then led to the porch and the front door.

Wallace stopped about half-way to the building and looked it over. Reyes went up the steps that led to the porch. He heard Wallace call out from several feet behind him.

'Are you the manager?'

'Yes. You're the police?'

Reyes showed his ID. 'I'm Detective Reyes. My partner back there is Detective Wallace. And you are?'

'I'm Josh Christie. I've called the owners and they are furious. They want to know when they can get access to the apartment in question.'

'We'll see what we can do once we've had a look inside.'

'What do you call the style of the building?' Wallace asked.

Christie's forehead creased in a frown. 'The style? It's ... er ... French Normandy.'

'It's painted an interesting shade of green.'

Wallace looked at the building. 'What do you call it?'

'What the hell? Are you a cop or a decorator?'

Reyes stood on the top step staring up at the manager. 'She's a cop. And she wants to know what color of green that is.'

'Myrtle. It's myrtle. The trim is oyster.'

'There. See how easy that was?' Reyes stepped onto the wooden porch. 'Do you want to show us Mr Pearl's apartment?'

'This Bart Pearl – he *is* the one whose body was found in that fire last night, isn't he?'

'He's the one.'

'The owners want to know how long before they can clear his stuff out. They're losing a great deal of money since he obviously won't be paying rent any longer.'

Reyes stared at the young man. Pearl was shot and barbecued and this prick was worried about rent. 'Maybe you should show us the apartment.'

'It's an absolute disaster. Once you're done, it will take several days before we can get it back to a satisfactory state.'

Reyes looked back at Wallace who smiled and nodded. *Another day, another dickhead.*

Christie led them down the hall to Apartment D. He opened the door and stepped aside. The place had been completely ransacked.

'Have you touched anything?' asked Reyes.

Christie shook his head.

'You sure?'

'I had a little walk through,' Christie admitted. 'Just to make sure no one was in here. You know?'

'Oh, I know,' said Reyes. He pulled a pair of latex gloves from his pocket and slowly moved into the room. 'Someone was looking for something beside loose change or a TV set.'

'I'm not a cop, but I'm pretty sure that they came in through that window.' Christie pointed to the open window in the kitchen. 'I think they broke in to vandalize the place. It looks like wanton destruction simply for the sake of it.'

'You're right.'

'I am?' Christie said.

'Yeah. You're not a cop. If you could wait here in the hall while we look around, that would be a good thing.'

'But...'

'Do you have any security in this place?' Reyes asked.

'We have a security camera and a concierge on duty twenty-four hours a day.'

'Really?' Wallace asked. 'I bet the tenants appreciate that.'

'They seem to, although this situation isn't going to help them feel any better.'

'Has Pearl been back recently?' said Reyes, steering his partner back to the scene.

'I hadn't seen him for a few months. We knew he was inside, but the rent was still being paid. Then the concierge saw him yesterday.'

'Why don't you go and find the tapes that correspond to that visit?' Reyes paused. 'Oh, and we'd like to talk to the dude on the desk, too.'

'Concierge,' Christie said as he was backed into the hall by the firm hand of Wallace pressing on his chest. She closed the door.

Under the rubble and ignoring the damage, the apartment was a classy place. Hardwood floors. Cove ceilings with fans. Leaded glass windows in the kitchen.

'I could see myself living in a place like this,' Wallace said.

'You looking to move?' Reyes asked. 'I think there's a vacancy.'

Wallace laughed. 'I don't think I could handle Josh every day.'

Reyes continued picking things up and dropping them again. Pillows were sliced open. Every painting was off the wall. The sofa had been turned over, the fabric covering the bottom was ripped off. 'Thorough,' Reyes said.

'That's an understatement,' said Wallace.

Reyes stepped over a floor lamp into the kitchen. Top to bottom, it was a chef's dream. Inset lighting. Over the counter lighting. Plenty of counter space. Brushed aluminum appliances. Lots of cabinets.

All the cabinets had been emptied by the intruder. Fortunately Pearl hadn't stocked up on much in the way of food. A couple of cans of soup. A box of chocolate chip cookies. Several microwavable meals-for-one. The fridge and freezer contained only a couple of beers and a quart of milk way past its use-by date.

While Wallace checked the food in the door of the refrigerator, Reyes poked a box of Rice Krispies that lay open and partially spilled on to the counter. He picked up the blue box. Another half cup of popped rice poured out of the box and hit the counter like hail, followed by a thump. 'What do we have here?' He picked up a small cellophane bag filled with white powder. 'Coke anyone?'

'Hardly enough to rip the joint apart for. Or to kill for.'

'There might have been more. Maybe they found the other bags.'

'Let's check the rest of the place.'

Room by room, Reyes and Wallace searched through the wreckage. Wallace rapped on the glass of one of the back bedrooms. 'This room would be perfect for a study.'

Reyes shook his head. *What is with her today?*

'You check the bathroom. I'll do the master bedroom.'

An overturned mattress presented a major hurdle. Reyes tugged it flat, half expecting to find a pool of blood underneath. Nothing. The drawers were out of the dresser, the closet turned inside out, and the contents of both were on the floor.

'Anything?' Wallace shouted from the bathroom.

'*Nada*. How about you?'

'Nothing. I don't think our boy met his end here. No kidding though, I like the apartment. They have tumbled marble tile in the bathroom. This grey-green is lovely.'

'Is there something you're not telling me, Phil?' Reyes said, putting his head around the bathroom door. 'You always have a keen eye for the crime scene but this is a little strange. You seriously thinking of getting a new place?'

Wallace stood with her feet firmly planted on a stack of crumpled towels. 'You know how things are. Some days are better than others.'

Reyes nodded. 'You want to talk about it?'

'I don't know. Things are kind of crappy, is all.'

'I can imagine. Having just one cop in the family makes things rough. Having two, well...' He waited but Wallace said nothing. 'Whatever is going on right now can't be helping things. I'd say wait until you and he both can wrap up your investigations and then see how you feel. Maybe whatever he's looking at is bothering him and...'

'Crooked cops, Sal.'

'What?' Reyes quickly digested the revelation. 'Oh shit. Not Brooks and Cresner?'

'I don't know.'

Reyes dusted off his hands. 'I'm not sure what I can ask.'

'Nothing. David told me nothing else.'

A voice called from the front of the apartment. 'Hello?'

'Back here,' Reyes said.

A man in his early fifties, pudgy, wearing a gray pinstripe off-the-rack suit, stepped into the hallway. 'Are you the two police officers investigating the break-in?'

'That would be us,' Wallace said. She showed her ID. 'That's Detective Reyes.'

'Mr Christie said you wanted to see me. My name is Bob Schaefer. I'm the concierge.'

'We'd like to ask you...'

'Oh, and some of our other tenants knew about the break-in.'

'Somebody knew about it?' Reyes asked.

'No. Sorry. I said that wrong. I asked around the building. Only the tenants from one other apartment heard or saw anything. I figured you would want to speak with them, so I brought them along.'

'You did?'

'They're in the hallway. Would you like to talk to them?'

'Yes,' said Wallace, 'I think we would. Could you wait until we finish with them?'

'Of course. Mr Christie is on the desk so I'm in no hurry. Let him see how hard I work.'

An elderly couple, long past retirement age, stood proudly together in the hall. She was dressed in a simple housecoat. His brown slacks were held up by suspenders.

'This is Mr And Mrs Beauchamp,' said Schaefer. He pointed to the next door along in the hall. 'They're the tenants from Apartment C.'

Wallace introduced herself and Reyes for the third time in half an hour.

'Could you tell me what you heard or saw yesterday as it regards this apartment's tenant?' asked Reyes.

'What'd he say?' Mr Beauchamp asked.

'He wants to know what we heard yesterday,' Mrs Beauchamp said.

'Why don't you tell them, Julianne,' Mr Beauchamp said. He continued to smile at Reyes and Wallace. 'You see officers, my hearing isn't so good anymore.'

'All right, why don't you tell us then Mrs Beauchamp?'

'It was eight o'clock. I remember because that's when Wilson – Mr Beauchamp,' she pointed a shaky finger at her husband, 'needs to take his medication. Every night at exactly eight, we have dessert, tea and Wilson takes his pills.'

'Last night was no different than any other night of your lives, right?' Wallace asked.

'That's correct. We heard the tea kettle whistle at five minutes to. I had finished setting up the tray and was on my way back to the dining-room – we were playing Scrabble you know – and there arose such a ruckus next door, I nearly dropped everything.'

'Go on,' Wallace said.

'That's all there is. Sometimes it was thump-thump,' she said, making her face into a frown and stomping on the floor. 'Sometimes it sounded like glass breaking. That bothered me, of course, but then things would get quiet again.'

'How long did the noise go on?' Reyes asked.

'I'm not sure, but I would say that the last significant sound I heard probably was around 8.40.'

And the last significant sound Mr Beauchamp heard was about thirty years ago, Reyes thought.

'Very good,' Wallace said. 'Was there anything else you heard or maybe saw?'

'That was all,' Mrs Beauchamp said. She turned to Mr Beauchamp. 'That was all, wasn't it, dear?'

'What? Oh, yes. That's right.' He nodded, looked at Reyes and Wallace. 'Two hundred and forty to one hundred and ninety-seven.'

'Pardon me?' Reyes said.

'She won.' Mr Beauchamp nodded at his wife.

'He thought you asked what the score of our Scrabble game was,' Mrs Beauchamp explained. 'His hearing, you know. It's not too good.'

Reyes smiled. 'Right. I remember that. Thank you both for coming forward.'

'Our pleasure,' she said. 'We heard what happened to the poor man that lived here. That Mr Pearl. It was all over the morning news.'

'It was horrible,' Mr Beauchamp said.

I wonder if he means Pearl's death or his losing the Scrabble game, Reyes thought.

The Beauchamps left. Schaefer looked at Reyes and Wallace. 'I assume it's my turn in the barrel, huh?'

'More or less,' Reyes said. 'Are there any security tapes?'

'Only in the lobby – it covers the desk and front door.'

'Is there another way in?'

'The garage entrance, used by maintenance, and also a door from the car park.'

'I've told your boss we'd like to check the tapes anyway,' said Reyes. 'And you were on duty yesterday, Mr Schaefer?'

'Yes, sir, from eight till eight.'

'Could you tell us what you saw or heard of Bartholomew Pearl?' asked Reyes.

129

'I was out on the porch enjoying a coffee break. Can't smoke inside you know, and I can't leave Security Post One, as I like to call it, the front desk. Well, who comes up but Mr Pearl. Kind of sneaky like. He asked if there had been anybody around looking for him. I said no. Then he says can I open up the underground maintenance garage door.'

'Underground?' Reyes asked.

'It's for our equipment. Lawn care stuff. We have a golf cart in there in case any of our guests are incapacitated. That sort of thing.'

'Did you let him in?'

'No. That area is for staff only. Besides, even if I wanted to, I couldn't leave my post to unlock it for him. I'd be fired in a heart-beat.'

'People usually didn't ask to do that kind of thing?'

'No. And it was doubly strange, because he came through the front door.'

'And why's that unusual?' said Wallace.

'Residents' parking is at the rear,' said Schaefer. 'Normally tenants come in through the back door.'

'So Pearl was on foot?' said Reyes.

'As far as I could tell,' Schaefer said. 'When I told him I couldn't let him in, he stormed off. He seemed, oh, I don't know, kind of pissed off. Or nervous? But to tell the truth, he was always that way. Agitated, I mean. I'd heard he was locked up on a

130

shooting charge.'

Reyes ignored the hint of a question in Schaefer's words. 'What time did Pearl show up?'

'It was during my coffee break so it had to be right around ten.'

'Thanks. If we need you, we know where to find you.'

Schaefer shuffled away, appearing none too eager to return to work.

Wallace paused in the hallway. 'What's up, Phil? You want to check the tape?'

'No, let a unit do it. I'd like to get a look at Simons' desk calendar again. I only noted two of the entries. Duke at seven in the morning and dinner at seven in the evening. It was at that new French place I was telling you about.'

'Oh yeah. Le Cochon qui Vole.' *The kind of place my ex would eat at.*

'That's the one. We need to find out who was coming to dinner and whether they all showed up. Then we have to find out who those other people were on his calendar, and track down Dwayne Duke, if indeed that is the person we're looking for.'

'Shouldn't we stick to the arson murder?' said Reyes. 'It's not like we need more work.'

'Okay, then tell me how we're supposed to investigate Pearl's murder? You know it overlaps with Simons' suicide – if it was a suicide – and if it doesn't get covered up.'

'Okay, come on, spill it. You know something.'

'I promised David I wouldn't tell anyone, so this has to be between us, okay?'

'Sure.'

Wallace leant back against the wall, her shoulders slumped. 'FID's investigation is focusing on two areas of concern – Wilshire and us. David told me it was about taking confiscated guns and selling them, but I think there's more. That shit with Cresner wasn't about guns. He was asking about Simons and Pearl. There's something else and it's dirty and deep. It's fucked up. We have to get past the FID troops and get some info out of that crime scene.'

'Damn, Phil. We're going to walk on razor blades if we push into the Simons' investigation.'

'Who do we know at the DA's office that can tell us why Pearl was out of jail in the first place?'

'Washington?'

'Great. Call him and see what he can tell you.'

Reyes pulled out his cell phone and called Darryl Washington.

'Hey, Darryl. It's Sal Reyes. How you been?'

'Good. Busy as hell.'

'Well, then, I won't take much of your time. I was wondering if you can you do me a favor? I'm working a couple of cases and I need some information on a con by the name of Bart Pearl...'

'Hold it. Sorry. Pearl's files are sealed. Only FID and the DA's office have access until further notice.'

'I don't want his file, I only need...'

'Dude. Off limits.'

'Okay. Okay. Who authorized the lock-down?'

'Barclay-Jones. You see my problem here, right?'

'Yeah. I understand. No sweat. See you around.'

Reyes passed the information, such as it was, to Wallace.

'The DA's office?' she asked.

'Yup. Sounds like the offer of support Barclay-Jones promised is no longer there.'

'If you can't get it from Washington and we can't get it from the DA's office, we aren't going to get it from anybody else in that chain of command.'

'Do you think FID had something to do with Pearl's release?'

'Twenty-four hours ago I would have said it was unlikely. Now, I'm not so sure. Bag up that coke. Let's tell Christie we're locking this place down until we can get forensics in here, then saddle-up.'

'Where we heading?'

'To jail, partner.'

133

12

'She's going to absolutely ruin the wedding, you know? Did you know that? Let me tell you her latest idea...'

Kahn's head drooped as he listened to Angie's rant. He had enough to worry about on his own side.

'...have you contacted your father yet?'

She must have read his mind.

'Er ... I'm on it, Angie, but y'know, I'm not sure it's a great idea.'

'We've spoken about this, hon. If you don't do it now, you never will.'

Don fought back the urge to say that was kind of his plan. He and his father hadn't spoken in years. Good old dad used to slap his mom around. His mother took it for years but then her health started to fail. The doctor gave her a prescription to help keep her calm. Within a few weeks she was sucking the pills down like candy.

'...red sashes,' Angie was saying. 'She wants the men to wear red sashes. Who does she think we are? Royalty?'

On Kahn's eighteenth birthday, he and his father stood eyeball to eyeball in the kitchen while his mother wept at the table through blackened eyes. His father stormed out. Within six months, Kahn's mother was dead from a drug overdose. Accidental, they said. A few months' later, Kahn was in the marines. Conversations with his father stopped.

The in-house line rang. 'Angie, I gotta go. I've got another call. Don't worry about your mother. We'll work it out somehow, okay? See you tonight.'

'I love you.'

Kahn glanced around. 'I love you, too.'

He punched the flashing line on his desk phone. 'Kahn.'

Ten seconds later, he stood up and looked over the cubicle wall. 'Harlen, we're wanted again.'

'Now what?'

'I don't know. Siley said to report to his office.'

'Man. That doesn't sound good.'

'If you didn't keep roughing people up, we wouldn't have to keep doing this.'

'It was you who broke the kid's arm, not me.'

'He looked like Santana,' Kahn said, in a high-pitched mocking voice.

'Stick it. At least one of those fuckers had a gun. If we hadn't been lucky, they'd be writing up our eulogies right about now. I hate this part of the job with a purple passion. How the hell ... aw, forget it.'

Standing at the corner of the Pit and the

hallway was a stout, tough-looking guy with a crew cut. 'Man, are you people slow. I'm talking Grandma-with-a-walker slow.'

'What the hell are you doing here, Krajcek?' Wagner asked.

'If you planned on squandering your Christmas bonus on something silly, forget it. The grandmother of that kid you beat the hell out of says she's going to sue.'

'There's a stunner, huh?' Kahn said.

'No bonuses this year?' Wagner said. 'Dang. I'll have to live off the money I took from you in the Super Bowl.'

'Come on, Harlen, we've got to go.'

'My boss is in with your boss.' Krajcek turned and walked down the hall with them. 'Let me warn you that they aren't exchanging recipes for fruit cake.'

Kahn stepped up to the Captain's door and tilted his head to hear the shouted conversation inside.

'What's he saying?' Wagner whispered.

'Captain Nader said Narcotics isn't taking the fall for and I quote, "Kahn and Wagner's over-exuberance".' He knocked on the door.

'Come in!' bellowed Siley.

Kahn went in, followed closely by his Wagner and Krajcek. Captain Siley sat behind his desk, looking like a man who had been given an enema and was feeling it start to work. Captain Nader sat in the farthest chair from the door. He was twisted slightly, looked over his left shoulder and cast a disparaging look their way. Captain Mangan, the officer Kahn had met at Cresner's party, sat in the other chair, a mischievous smile on his puss.

'Don. Harlen. You both know Captain Nader, Deputy Chief of Narcotics? And Captain Mangan from Vice? Now that everybody knows everybody else, you want to close the door, sergeant?'

Krajcek closed the door and leaned with his back against it.

Does he think we gonna run? thought Kahn.

He shuffled with Wagner off to the right side of Siley's desk, as close to the wall as they could get. Siley stared on them. 'You know we've been doing our damndest to avoid controversy in this department. We had a lot of bad publicity to overcome from some errors made months ago. Somehow, we managed to do that. Now, between the FID investigation and your kicking the crap out of a teenager, we're getting unwanted attention. It's up to me to try and deflect some of that heat.'

Kahn looked at Mangan, whose pose hadn't changed. Nader was picking at his fingernails, as though the whole affair bored him. Kahn was dreading what might be said next. *You're back on foot patrol.* No, they wouldn't do that. The detective squad was already light.

Siley leaned back in his chair, folded his hands and rested them on his chest. 'Captain Mangan informs me that due to a staff shortage in Vice, he is looking for a couple of volunteers for temporary assignment. I am sure that you two will be eager to help him out.'

'You want us to work with Vice?' Kahn said. 'That's it?'

'Yes,' Siley said. 'And a reduction of pay for two months.'

'Aw, bullshit,' Wagner said. 'If this is because of that punk kid, his arm got broken resisting arrest. They fired shots at us, for fuck's sake. Why should we be punished for that?'

'The doctor said there were numerous bruises on his body and head.'

'I mentioned those in my report, Captain,' said Kahn. 'The kid resisted.'

'The kid's five-nine, and you two are both old and big enough to know better,' said Siley.

Wagner gave Kahn a 'what-can-you-do?' look.

'However,' Siley said, 'If FID clears you of abuse of a suspect, I'll drop the fines.'

'Thanks, captain,' Kahn said.

'Unfortunately for you two, FID is a bit tied up right now. So...'

Kahn sighed. 'What in particular does Vice need us for?'

'We're doing a prostitution sting,' Mangan said. 'We're more interested in the johns than the hookers this time.'

'Anybody in particular you're looking for?' Wagner asked.

'We'll sort 'em out when we get 'em,' Mangan said. 'Sergeant Krajcek's group is handling the operation.'

'Hell, I might even know a few of the ladies on a first-name basis.'

'Wagner,' Siley said, raising a warning finger.

'I'm not saying I'm a client, captain, but I do know how to work the street. So maybe the ladies can help me find whoever it is you're looking for.'

Mangan's grin returned. 'It'll be nice to have your expertise. I think Captain Siley forgot to mention that this sting is focusing on male prostitution.'

Kahn went stiff, and Wagner looked like he had when he found out the Precinct summer party was alcohol-free.

'We need you to go undercover,' Mangan said.

'Undercover? Wait a minute,' Wagner said. 'Are you saying you want us to dress like some faggot? You want us to be queer bait?'

'That's not the way I'd put it, but yes,' Mangan said. 'We need you to do a little booty-shaking.' Siley was chuckling to himself and Krajcek was grinning from ear to ear.

'Not me, man.' He turned to Kahn. 'You're more feminine, partner.'

Kahn's stare down slammed that door. 'I

think they already selected you for the role.'

'Crap. Okay,' said Wagner. 'I'm a professional; I'll take one for the team.'

Krajcek stepped forward. 'We should mention, any body part that's exposed has to be clean. The johns are looking to experience that young boy feel. They aren't looking to fuck some hairy-assed mother.'

Wagner shook his head. 'No way am I shaving my body hair.'

Siley stood up. 'I think we're done here. It's two o'clock. What time do you need them over there, Captain Mangan?'

'Any time. We can get some practice in.'

'Practice?' Wagner squirmed. 'What kind of practice?'

'You have to know how to act. How to use the equipment. What to say to the johns. That kind of thing.'

'You two get over to Vice as soon as you can, then,' said Siley. 'If you have anything that needs tending to here, any loose ends, let one of the others know before you go.'

Wagner left the room quickly and headed straight for the back door. Kahn followed. He knew his partner needed a cigarette. He probably wanted a drink, too, but since they had to report to Vice, he might resist the temptation.

Kahn shoved the door to the outside open and headed for their favorite smoking spot – under the tree.

'Here,' Wagner offered him his pack of cigarettes.

'GPCs? What happened to the Marlboros?'

'I got a buy one, get one free coupon. I figured what the hell. They aren't bad. Go ahead, try one.'

Kahn took one and handed the pack back. 'This is not a good time for me to be hit in the wallet,' he said, as he lit the cigarette. 'I'm trying to put aside some money for the wedding.'

'I thought the women paid for the wedding. You know, out of gratitude.' Wagner laughed. 'Sorry. Couldn't help myself.'

'Angie is paying for a lot of it. I still have expenses. We're renting a hall. I think we are anyway. Her mom may have changed that again since I left for work.'

'Why don't you tell that nosy bitch to stay out of it?'

'Yeah, right. I'm going to tell Angie's mom to butt out of her daughter's wedding.'

'I would.'

'Not if you hoped to get married, you wouldn't. Attacking the mom is the worse thing you can do.'

'What other expenses do you have?'

'The bar.'

'I told you before that I can help with that. I'll get my buddy over at Roget's to give me a deal.'

'Really?'

'I'm your best man, aren't I? Now what else do you need help with?'

'The honeymoon.'

'I can help there, too.' He smiled. 'I mean, after all, isn't that why they call me the best man?'

'Stay classy, partner. I'm talking money, not romance. But speaking of screwing, did I ever tell you that I had a friend who was a male prostitute?

'For real?'

'He was hung like a bull, but unfortunately he contracted leprosy and his business fell off.'

13

DODGER STADIUM – 1 mile.

The green information sign that hung over the 101 reminded Reyes of the missed opportunities to be with his son last season. As if reading his mind, Wallace said, 'You're a Dodger's fan, aren't you Sal?'

'Yeah.'

'You ever get tickets from Captain Siley? He's got box seats.'

'He gave me a pair last year. I called Pam to see if she would let me take Fernando, even though it wasn't one of my official visit days. It was last minute and the tickets were for that night. I don't have to tell you she said "no".'

'Why is she like that?'

'I don't know. I'm hoping that getting married again might change her attitude.'

'You don't really care if she gets married again though, right?'

'No. Why would I give a shit?'

'You sure?'

Reyes looked at Wallace. 'Are you serious?'

'You know the old saying, *You don't know what you've got till it's gone?*'

'Not in my case.' Reyes turned and looked at his partner. 'We were talking about me, right?'

Wallace smiled. 'Here's our exit,' she said, pointing at the information sign: *Men's Central Jail. Exit ¼ mile.*

'You're pretty sure the FID hasn't contacted anyone in the Sheriff's department, right?'

'I doubt it. FID is internal.' Wallace turned south on North Vignes Street. 'I doubt David's troops even give a shit about some penny ante thug who happened to share a cell with Pearl. That's why they do what they do and we do what we do.'

'Don't go to the regular lot. Go down Bauchet. Less walking.'

'Anything that saves my poor dogs is fine with me.'

'What kind of story are you going to tell the guys inside? Or are you going with the truth?'

They found a parking place and Wallace killed the engine. 'I'm going to tell them my version of the truth.'

'Sounds good. I'll smile and nod and mumble something in Spanish, like *"Yo no hablo inglés"*.'

'Come on, smart ass.'

Wallace and Reyes walked shoulder-to-shoulder across the parking lot. They checked their guns and signed in at the reception desk. A Sergeant Ehling came out of his office and looked at their IDs. The buttons of his shirt were straining against his impressive girth. 'So, what can we do for you, detectives?'

'We're looking into a homicide. The vic's name was Bartholomew Pearl. He was housed here for some time.'

Ehling eyed them a little suspiciously. Reyes knew his type: only ever got off his ass for a Twinkie.

'Yeah, that the guy they found up on St Andrew's?'

'It certainly is,' said Wallace. 'Can you tell us when he was released?'

There was a slight pause. 'Yesterday morning. First thing.'

'You don't think it's a little strange that he was dead by the afternoon?'

'Hey,' said Ehling. 'My business ends

when I turf these pricks out.'

Reyes stepped forward, trying not to lose his patience. 'So you don't know why a scumbag who shot a cop walked out of here?'

Ehling eyed the badge at Reyes' waist. '*Detective*, I don't like your tone.'

The officer sitting at the desk looked up, suddenly interested.

Wallace used a more conciliatory tone. 'Sorry, sergeant. We've got two probable homicides, and the shit's really hit the fan. The cop Pearl shot was a colleague of ours.'

Reyes managed a smile, held up his hand and backed off.

'Who gave the order to release Pearl?' asked Wallace.

Ehling passed a dirty handkerchief over his brow. 'The only people who could. The DA's office.'

'Do you know why?'

'I guess he must have cut a deal of some sort. They met in private.'

'I see,' said Wallace. 'Sergeant, did Pearl have a cell to himself?'

'You're joking, right. This ain't the Beverly Hilton.'

'Could we have a word with his former cellmate?'

'I don't see why not. Fred,' Ehling spoke to the officer at the desk, 'can you assist these detectives, please?'

The officer tapped at his keyboard, his

145

eyes scrolling the screen.

'Pearl was in with Ducker, H.'

'Get him into one of the interview rooms. Show these two detectives where to go. Detectives, I'll leave you in the capable hands of Officer Robbins.'

'Thanks, sergeant,' Wallace said. 'You've been a great help.'

After Ehling had waddled back into his office, Robbins showed Wallace and Reyes into an interview room. 'We'll get Ducker down in a few minutes.'

The room was small. White cement block walls. Four chairs. One table. Reyes took a seat.

Wallace began pacing. 'Here's something that is bothering me. The DA got Pearl out of jail. So then, why turn right around and issue an All Points Bulletin?'

'I heard that he was supposed to report back and didn't show.'

'And that makes sense to you? Have you ever heard of that kind of deal before, where they let a guy out and then try to get him back?'

'They do that kind of thing all the time. They call them compassionate leaves. Like, if the guy's mom is dying or something. If they let him out and he promises to come back and doesn't, they put out an APB.'

'Sal. Come on.' Wallace shook her head. 'Central houses the majority of Los Angeles

County's high risk, high security inmates. You don't let that kind of inmate waltz out to go visit Grandma.'

'If Cresner had died, I agree. But since he was only wounded, I bet a smart lawyer could swing a release for Pearl – at least a temporary one.'

The door opened and a man in his mid-twenties with muddy-colored hair and the face of an altar boy shuffled in. He was escorted by his jailer who looked like his last job was in the movie *Deliverance*.

'You the folks looking for Ducker?' the jailer asked. He scratched his nose. 'I never got a request in writing. I usually get some kind of memo, don't ya know?'

Reyes smiled. 'It was a last minute thing. Say, you have a unique accent there, uh, Officer Bass, is it? Where are you from originally?'

'E-ya. Orville Bass. You never heard of where I'm from. It's a small place called Frog Croak, Georgia.'

'Unusual name. Well, thanks for bringing Mr Ducker down. We only have a few questions for him. If you would step out of the room, please.'

'Sure. Take your time.' He strolled from the room and closed the door behind him.

'My name is Detective Wallace,' Wallace said, turning to Ducker. 'My partner is Detective Reyes. I didn't catch your first name.'

'Harry.'

'Well, Harry, we'd like to ask you a few questions about one of your former cell-mates, Bartholomew Pearl.'

'Okay.'

'You two shared a cell until his release a yesterday. Is that correct?'

'Yes.' His gaze never locked on either detective but wandered all over, finally focusing on the table top where he scraped at something unseen by Reyes.

'Just you and Pearl?' he asked.

'Yes.'

'Did he say anything to you about his release?'

'Yes.'

The room was hot, with no air-con, and Reyes could feel the sweat pushing through his pores. 'If you think this one-word answer shit is cute, you're dead wrong. We can turn some screws and make your life inside a living hell.'

Ducker looked at Reyes for the first time. 'If I tell you anything and the others find out, I'm a dead man. I ain't blessed like Pearl was. I've got three new roommates since he got out.'

'No one is going to find out anything. We're the only ones working this case. I'm not writing anything down. No record. Okay?'

'Get me ten packs of smokes at least.'

'Guaranteed. Now, tell me about Pearl.

What did you mean that he was blessed?'

'You know – he had a guardian angel.'

'You're saying he was protected?'

Ducker nodded. 'So he said.'

'And you believed him?'

'Hey, I wasn't sharing with three others back then. He was happy, I was happy.'

Reyes shared a look with Wallace. This was like getting blood out of a stone.

'And did this angel spring him?' asked Reyes.

'I guess so,' Ducker replied. 'Bart agreed to flip on somebody. He never said who, but somebody wanted his info pretty bad.'

'He was going to testify against somebody? Who?'

'I have no idea. Pearl was in shit with everybody, at least that's how he talked. He said he was cutting a deal and they were going to let him loose. I don't think Pearl planned on coming back ever. He walked out of here and within ten minutes, the guards were in my cell cleaning out his shit, stripping the bed and stuff. Thirty minutes after that, I've got three more roommates.'

'Isn't it kind of odd that he told you he was cutting a deal? That makes him a snitch and snitches don't fare too well inside. He wouldn't go bragging about it to you or anybody else. He'd wait for his release and vanish.'

'Pearl and me shared that cell from the

149

first day he got here, about three months ago. The other guy in the cell the morning Pearl arrived, Sly Conover, was serving life for murder. He scared the hell out of me. I slept with one eye open and hoped he wouldn't pluck it out.

'The guards came, pulled him out and put Pearl in. I'm going to tell you that Conover was pissed. He had been in that same cell for years. It was his home. He told me I was his guest. Anyway, the word spread that he was going to take Pearl out.'

'And what happened?'

'Twenty-four hours later, Conover got the shit beat out of him in his new cell.'

'By Pearl?'

'No. Pearl was no pussy, but Conover would have killed him in a straight-up fight. What we heard was that Pearl had a friendly cop on the outside who could pull strings. After the beating, Pearl was given a wide berth by everyone, including Conover.'

'I don't suppose he ever mentioned this cop's name?' Wallace chipped in.

'Nope.' Ducker looked at Wallace and motioned that she move closer, to join the group. In a whisper he said 'Someone smuggled in stuff for Pearl. He got some crack. He got me cigarettes. I think that was so I'd keep my mouth shut.'

'The name Cresner mean anything to you?'

'I think so.' Reyes found he was holding

his breath. 'No. Wait. Wasn't that the cop who Pearl plugged?'

Wallace nodded. 'We'll see that you get some cigarettes. What kind do you smoke?'

'I don't care. Some kind of menthol. I usually trade most of them for other stuff.'

'I'll get them to you.'

'Maybe I should tell people I have two cops who are my guardian angels.'

'I wouldn't do that if I were you,' Reyes said.

'Can't blame a guy for asking.'

Wallace nodded to him, and Reyes stepped into the hall with her. Deputy Bass entered the room to retrieve the prisoner. Reyes half expected to hear banjo music.

'Come on, Sal,' Wallace said. 'I want to see who visited Pearl. If this character who was Pearl's guardian angel came down here to talk to him, he would have had to sign in.'

'Good thinking. Of course, if the guy is working inside the prison, he wouldn't have to sign in.'

'No harm in trying.'

They stopped back by Sergeant Ehling's office to pick up their weapons and sign out. The sergeant was out. 'Officer Robbins,' Wallace said, 'could we see the visitor records for Pearl?'

'Sure,' Robbins said. He retrieved a binder from the book shelf, opened it and flipped to the Ps. He thumbed through a few pages.

151

'Paxson. Pauly. Pearl. Here he is.' Robbins laughed. 'Apparently he didn't have too many friends.' He handed the plastic three-ring binder to Wallace.

She took it and gasped. 'Oh, shit.'

'What's the matter?' Reyes asked.

'There are only two names.' Her voice was sombre. 'The first one is 'Arson ... no it's Arsenio. Yeah. Arsenio Ignatiez. He came by twice right after Pearl was arrested.'

'Who the hell is that?'

'I don't know. We'll find out. It's the second guy that bothers me.'

'Giordano?'

'I wish it was. Here.' She handed the binder to Reyes.

'Okay, Ignatiez, Ignatiez again and...' Reyes raised his head and stared at Wallace. 'This is some kind of mess.'

The second name was Raymond Brooks.

14

Wallace sat scrunched behind the wheel of the car as she and Reyes drove back down the 101 toward the station. 'I'm having trouble putting all the pieces together and making sense of them. Every time we try to clear up one question, we seem to raise two more.

Now, why in the hell would Brooks visit Pearl?'

'You know why,' Reyes said.

'Then give me *other* reasons why he would visit Pearl in jail.'

'Ones that don't make him look guilty?'

'I've known the man my whole career. There is no way he turned. No way.'

Reyes gazed at the cars they passed. 'Come on, Phil. Why do you think FID talked to Brooks and Cresner?'

'Hell, I don't know. Brooks is Cresner's buddy. Maybe Cresner's mixed up in something and they thought Ray knew something.'

'Phil, if Brooks wasn't a friend, he'd be number one on your suspect list. Pearl had a guardian angel – a cop – who was also smuggling in dope. Only two people visited Pearl. Only one of those two is a cop. Well, at least we think so. Let me run the other guy.'

Reyes turned the computer and typed in the name. Wallace glanced over at the photo.

'Skinny-looking dude.'

'Not bad for a dead man, though.' Reyes pointed to the status line.

'Dead?'

'The report says he was found dead in front of Hamilton's Home Appliances on East Sixth. Shot.'

'When?'

'About four weeks ago. Unsolved, but

suspected drug-related.'

'Do we have anything else on him?'

'It looks like he was a two-bit pusher. Numerous arrests, two convictions. Possession. Assault in a bar fight. He could be our drug mule.'

'How in the hell did a convicted dope-dealing felon get access to an addict in jail who was awaiting trial for shooting a cop? That's beyond comprehension.'

'Pearl's guardian angel?'

'Had to be. When we get back, I'm going to get Brooks on the side and see what he can tell us.'

'I'd be careful, Phil. The way he reacted in the OR about us listening in on Cresner – I've never seen him get so angry. I mean, he was pissed. He didn't want to hear anyone suggest that Cresner was dirty. If you confront him, he's going to take it as an attack on his own character. That kind of thing could linger in his gut for a long time.'

'Maybe you're right, but I have to do something.'

Wallace thought hard about Brooks. Reyes was one hundred per cent correct. Talking to him about his visit to Pearl was risky enough as far as their friendship went. She'd get his back up, sure as shit. Also, if she talked to Brooks about the investigation, there was a good chance word would get back to FID. David's bosses would probably want to know if he leaked information to her. He would be furious, claiming she was interfering in his job. And that wasn't the kind of thing you could leave at the office.

'Let's go over a few things,' she said. 'Ducker said Pearl bought his way out of jail by giving somebody up. What if all those jobs Pearl Construction was awarded were the result of a little bribery? And what if Pearl offered to turn state's evidence against Simons?'

'So Simons takes out Pearl, then tops himself.'

'Been there, done that. Simons doesn't go to the length of carrying out an intricate murder, carrying the body across town from God knows where, only to sit at his desk and kill himself. There is another possibility. Davey's wife was bitching about someone downtown trying to screw her husband over because he won't play their games. What if Davey found out about the bribes and killed them both?'

'Look at Sam Davey, Phil. He's not a killer.' Wallace took a left. 'Hey, the station's that way.'

'If we're going to keep checking things out, then let's swing by Le Cochon qui Vole and see if we find out who Simons was seeing that night.'

'It won't hurt to ask, I guess, but it's doubtful.'

'Why doubtful?'

'Because reservations are in one person's name – the person making them. Reyes and a party of five. That kind of thing.'

Reyes checked his watch. 'It's almost three. Maybe we can grab a sandwich or something.'

'Sure, though I don't know if your pay-packet extends that far.'

Thirty minutes later Wallace and Reyes pulled up at two-twenty-four South Beverly Drive and got out.

Wallace took a look at the building and the people milling around outside who were waiting for a table. Two young ladies dressed in what could just be described as a uniform stood to either side of a sign that read *Valet Parking*. They wore tux jackets with black shorts and white calf-high boots. The rest of the people looked shabby compared to the two valet attendants.

Reyes opened the door.

The lobby area was dark. Modern sculpted sofas. Stylized mirrors, decorated with frills and etchings. Impressionist prints. The walls were dark-red.

'Ahem. I'm afraid the wait is nearly an hour,' the shiny-headed *maitre d'* said. 'Do you still wish to be placed on the list?' He tapped his pen on the podium impatiently.

'What if we've reservations?' Reyes asked.

'Do you have reservations?'

'I think we do.' Reyes flipped out his identification card.

The *maitre d'* looked around nervously. In a hushed voice he asked, 'What can I do for you?'

'We need to talk to the person in charge.'

He turned to a young female employee standing to his right. 'Antoinette. Please take these – special guests – to the manager's office.'

'This way,' a petite young waitress said, in a French accent. 'Monsieur Perrault's office is in the back.'

'Are you French?' Reyes asked.

She smiled. 'No. They like us to use a little French when we can. I took French in high school, so I can fake it better than some of the others.' She paused outside of the door marked with a plate that said *Manager*. 'My name isn't even really Antoinette.'

She knocked on the door, waited for an acknowledgement, and opened it. 'Monsieur Perrault. These are *gendarmes*. Monsieur Leggett said to bring them back to see you.'

'*Gendarmes?*' The man behind the desk rose to his full height of five foot five. 'Oh. Police. Right. *Merci*, Antoinette. I will handle it from here. Please come in, officers.'

Wallace introduced herself and Reyes.

'You received reservations for dinner at

seven last night from a city council member called Theodore Simons.'

'Perhaps,' Perrault said. 'We receive dinner reservations every night from many of the influential residents of Los Angeles.'

'Well, we know he didn't show,' Wallace said. 'We'd like to know if anyone did?'

'I believe we can handle your request, detective. Confidentially, of course.'

'Oh, but of course.'

Perrault sat down, picked up the phone and punched a single key. He waited only a few seconds. 'Did you take a reservation for Mr Simons last night?' He looked up and gave a tight grin. 'For seven o'clock? Table? Nine. Thank you.' He replaced the phone and spun around, facing a computer on his credenza. 'Come around,' Perrault said as he checked his watch for the date. Without a word, he opened a drawer, pulled out a plastic jewel case, one of many, removed the disc and inserted it into the player. Wallace and Reyes stood behind him and watched the screen.

Perrault hit a number of keys on the keyboard and a few seconds later, with a faint whir, the screen brought up a video. The time 19.00 flashed in the upper left hand corner of the screen. 'Table nine, seven pm last night.'

Wallace stared at the screen as figures blurred past each side of the table in fast forward. 19.01. 19.02. 19.03. At seven minutes after seven, a waiter seated a lone male. Perrault slowed the footage. As the waiter handed over a menu, the man briefly lifted his face toward the camera.

'Sonny Giordano,' said Reyes. 'That's our link.'

'Let's keep watching,' Wallace said. 'See if anyone else shows up.'

Perrault sped up the action again, and Wallace watched as the video zipped ahead twenty minutes, thirty minutes. At 19.40 Giordano appeared to place his order. Twenty-two minutes passed and the waiter brought his dinner. At 8.50, after three courses, Giordano finished dining – alone. He drank his coffee, checked his watch, then paid the bill and left.

'Can you burn us a copy of the footage?' Reyes asked.

'Anything to be of service,' said Perrault. 'May I ask, is there some problem? I'd rather the restaurant didn't receive any ... bad publicity.'

'You can ask,' said Wallace. 'Your cooperation is appreciated, Mr Perrault.'

A few minutes later, Wallace and Reyes were outside and heading for their car, a copy of the security film in Reyes' hand.

Reyes settled into his seat. 'Are you confused, Phil?'

'Things have gotten kind of fuzzy, all right.'

'Fuzzy? This case is getting crazier by the

minute. The brother-in-law of the fire victim who, by the way, should still have been in jail, is going to have dinner with a guy who kills himself not long after breakfast. We're allowed to investigate the arson homicide, but the FID runs roughshod over us when it comes to looking at the suicide.' He took a breath. 'Which may have been a homicide.'

'Call in and ask them to have a unit pick up Giordano.'

'You think he killed Simons? I can't believe he would have killed Simons and then kept his dinner engagement.'

'If he was smart, he'd keep the appointment. Only someone who knew Simons was dead wouldn't show up to have dinner with him.'

'Good point.'

'I also think he lied to us. I think he was trying to use us to settle an old grudge against Davey. Now, I'd like to see if we could get him to tell us what he does know.'

'How about two for one?'

'How's that?'

'I'd like to hear what his wife knows about the situation.' Reyes picked up the radio. 'After all, it was her brother who was killed and you know what they say about blood being thicker than water.'

Wallace nodded. 'Yeah, that's what I hear.'

15

Back in the break room at Wilcox Avenue, Reyes jammed half a cookie into his mouth and shot the wrapper toward the wastebasket. 'Good for three.'

'Think the NBA could use a five-foot-eight Mexican shooting guard?' said Wallace.

'Let me see how this cop thing works out first,' Reyes replied.

Officer Jaworski had taken Sonny Giordano to IR One and his wife, Rita into a separate room. Both had come in without much trouble, on the basis of helping the investigation into Pearl's death, though Jaworski had said he detected a hint of resistance in Sonny. Wallace was cursing the coffee-pot in low tones.

'You want to take one and me the other, or what?'

'Nah. Let's do it together.'

'If there was any bribery involved, Giordano sure as hell should know about it. After that, we don't have much.'

'If we get close, maybe one of them will spill something. As one of my friends used to say, if you can't dazzle them with your brilliance, baffle them with your bullshit.'

'I don't know if that's going to work with Sonny. We might be able to con the wife, though. Maybe we can convince her that hubby had her brother killed.'

'Let's go with the flow.'

Reyes retrieved the pertinent files and joined Wallace at the IR. She threw open the door to Interview Room One and took a seat across from Giordano. Reyes stepped in and reached for the door. Before he could close it, Giordano started spouting off.

'It's about damn time you guys got in here. I'm a busy man.'

'Yeah, well, depending on how things go in the next thirty minutes or so, you may not be so busy for a long time to come.'

'What's that supposed to mean?'

Wallace took a folder from the stack Reyes had brought into the room. She flipped it open. Inside were several photos of Ted Simons sitting dead at his desk and the restaurant CD in a case. Wallace placed the photos on the table, allowing Giordano a few seconds to check them out. She picked up the jewel case and pointed it at Giordano. 'This is footage we obtained from the security cameras at Le Cochon qui Vole. Do you know who's on it?'

Giordano stared at the plastic case but said nothing.

'Playing stupid isn't going to help you very much. You know damn good and well who's on it, don't you, Mr Giordano?'

'Okay. So I ate dinner at a trendy restaurant. Big deal.'

'You dined alone?'

'You've got the film. Did I?'

'The table was set for two. Who didn't show? And if you hope to go home today, cut the bullshit.'

Wallace was good. Giordano paused, most likely considering whether having dinner in any way constituted a crime. 'Okay, so what? I was supposed to have dinner with a friend who happens to be a councilman. They're allowed to have friends, aren't they?'

'In this case, there are two unique things about the council member. The first is that he approved construction bids. He approved a boat-load of them for Pearl Construction in the last five years. The second thing unique to him was that he was whacked a few hours before you two were supposed to have dinner.'

'Whacked?'

Wallace slammed her hand on the table. 'I said cut the bullshit.'

'Who did it?'

'Cute,' said Reyes. 'Were you the one bribing him?'

'I don't know what the fuck you're talking about.'

'Of course you don't,' said Wallace. 'And if we subpoena your bank details, your wife's bank details, and your brother-in-law's, and cross-reference them with the contract dates, we won't find anything at all.'

'What do you expect to find?'

'I think you know, Sonny. You've heard of asset forfeiture, yes?'

'So what?'

'Well, if we find your business dealings with the council are anything but one hundred and ten per cent watertight, we take your house in lieu. You got that? We can take whatever we want.'

'I told you. I know nothing about any kick-backs.'

'I didn't mention kickbacks, Sonny,' said Wallace. 'I think you need to start talking.'

Giordano blinked nervously. 'You said this was about bribery.'

Reyes walked behind him, and spoke in a low voice. 'You think business is going to be good if every week we get a couple of uni-forms following you around, turning up at sites, interrupting meetings. Checking every fucking letter of every contract that passes your desk. Making sure all your hard-hats are regulation, that sort of thing...'

'Hey, man, that's blackmail,' said Gior-dano, twisting in his seat to look at Reyes. 'Are you recording this?'

'It's the law, Sonny,' said Wallace. 'My partner isn't joking. Just tell us about these kickbacks, and we'll leave you alone. It was

Bart, wasn't it?'

Giordano looked to the side, chewed his lip, then snapped his eyes back. He nodded.

'Yeah, it was Bart,' Giordano said. 'I didn't have anything to do with any of that shit.'

Behind him, Reyes grinned.

'So, you're saying it was all Pearl's idea? He handled it?'

'Yeah ... I ...'

'Your brother-in-law bought his freedom by cutting a deal. He promised to testify against somebody, didn't he Sonny?'

Giordano shook his head. 'I don't know. I haven't seen Bart since he went in. I don't...'

'This isn't rocket science. He walked out of jail and within forty-eight hours, both he and Simons are dead. It's kind of obvious.'

'It is?'

'Come on, Sonny. Who gains the most by eliminating Pearl?'

'I don't know, who?'

'You'd take over his company, wouldn't you?'

'You think I killed Bart? Where's Rita?'

'Here's what we know,' Reyes said. 'Tell us what you think. Pearl was bribing Simons to give your construction company an edge. His drug habit was crippling him inside Central so he agreed to squeal – expose the whole crooked mess – but only if he could walk. He sold everyone out for a fix. When he called you, you knew that if word got around about the bribes, Pearl Construction would be forced out of business. Finished. Kaput. Lawsuits up the ying-yang. You'd be charged with half a dozen crimes. The great life you busted your hump to build would be gone, and all because of your brother-in-law.'

'There was only one way out, right Sonny?' Wallace said, drawing Giordano's focus back to her. 'The only way to prevent all of that from happening, was to take him out. A dead man can't testify.'

They'd gone too far, and Giordano visibly relaxed, sitting back in his seat. 'Bart was family,' he said.

'You're breaking my heart,' Wallace leaned closer. 'You were so close to good old Bart that the entire time he was awaiting trial, you didn't even stop by to say hello. The man was probably climbing the walls with that drug habit of his, but you and your wife did absolutely nothing for him. You didn't even bring the guy a Hershey bar.'

'Wait a minute. The only reason I took over his part of the operations was because he got arrested. I couldn't trust anybody else, but we had too many contracts for one guy to handle. I didn't have time...'

'All contracts approved by Simons,' muttered Wallace, just loud enough for Giordano to hear.

'What did Rita have to do with all of this?'

Reyes cut in.

Giordano scratched his head. 'Rita?'

'Yeah. You do remember your wife don't you – Rita?'

'She doesn't know anything.'

'So you're trying to say that you were in this alone? That's not the impression I got,' Reyes said. 'How about you, Phil? Is that the impression you got?'

'Not by a long shot.'

'What did she say?' Giordano said. 'I don't even understand why you're interrogating her.'

'No, no. We don't interrogate. We were interviewing her. Seriously, where did you think we were all this time, having coffee?' Reyes said. 'You know what, Phil? Maybe we should go back and talk to Rita again.' He pushed back from the table. 'Maybe she can clear some of the confusion up for us.'

'I agree,' Wallace said, as she stood up. She handed the CD and photos of Simons back to Reyes. 'You sit tight. We'll be back.'

'Rita didn't do anything and she doesn't know anything.' His eyes searched the faces of both detectives. 'Come on, the woman just found out that her brother was murdered. Give her a break.'

'I'm ready.' Reyes stood, picked up the folders and opened the door.

'What do you want from me?' Giordano asked.

Wallace walked out. Reyes stood quietly by the door for a moment looking at Giordano. 'I think you underestimate your wife.'

Reyes pulled the door shut behind him before Giordano could respond. 'Well, that seemed to go well.'

'He confirmed your suspicions about Simons taking bribes. We need to get that in writing. Man, would I like to get into Simons' office again.'

'FID won't let us near any of the Simons information. Unless you can get David to...'

'No. Let's go talk to Mrs Giordano.'

Brooks walked toward them carrying a folder. He looked angry and tired. 'If you didn't hear, Hackett confirmed Pearl didn't die in the fire. He was killed somewhere else and dumped there. No smoke in the lungs. He was shot in the head. One round to the right temple. Close range. Thankfully, the bullet lodged in the skull.'

'Any ballistics?' said Reyes.

Brooks opened the file, turned over a couple of pages, and ran his finger down the sheet.

'Nine by eighteen from a Makarov.'

16

Reyes took the folder. 'Okay, thanks, sarge.'

He looked at Brooks and wanted to say something but all he could come up with was, 'How are you doing?'

'Shitty.' Brooks turned and headed back toward his desk.

'He's finding it tough,' said Wallace.

Guilt rides a man hard, thought Reyes.

'Twenty bucks says it was same Makarov we found with Simons,' he said.

'No way we can find that out without stepping on FID's toes,' said Wallace. She'd already turned to Interview Room Two. 'Second verse, same as the first.'

Reyes followed her in. Rita Giordano was a petite, pretty redhead, though the strain was showing in the lines on her pale face. Her bony hands were clasped tightly in front of her, but now and then she flicked the hair from her face.

'There you are,' she said. 'I've been waiting a long time. Can you tell me why we're even here? Have you found Bart's killer?'

Reyes took the seat directly across from Rita Giordano. Wallace sat at the end of the table. 'We had to speak to your husband first,' Reyes said. 'He had some interesting things to say. We thought that maybe we should let you have a chance to defend ... I mean, we thought we should hear your side of things before we proceed.'

Rita looked confused. 'My side of things?'

'What role did you play in the business?'

'Me? I didn't do anything.'

Reyes opened a folder and flipped a few sheets. He ran his finger down as though he was reading and trying to locate the correct spot on the page. He jabbed his index finger on the paper. 'Ah, yes,' he said, as looked into her eyes. 'These bribes, Rita – they don't make Bart look like an angel, do they?'

'Bribes? I don't know anything about bribes. Who told you that?'

Reyes held up his hands as if to say that the information was confidential. He rolled his eyes toward the wall and what was on the other side of the wall.

'Sonny?'

Reyes looked back at the sheet as if to confirm what he had read. It was a bullshit bluff, but she had bitten on it. He shrugged. 'What can I say?'

'Something's wrong. I don't know who told you that, but it wasn't Sonny.'

'Why didn't you join your husband at dinner last night?' Wallace asked.

'He didn't invite me.'

'So you don't have an alibi for yesterday?'

'An alibi? Why do I need an alibi?'

'Come on, Rita. You and your husband had a lot to lose if the bribes came out. Only two other people knew about them, and now those two people are dead.'

She took a couple of short breaths and put her hand in front of her mouth. 'That no good councilman must have done it. He was always telling Bart what he could and couldn't do.'

'Simons was murdered too, Rita,' said Wallace, quietly.

Rita sat quietly for a few seconds, then quickly made the sign of the cross.

Reyes flipped another page in the file and pretended once again to read. This time he kept focused on the sheet in the folder. 'Sonny tells us that he and Bart didn't see eye to eye on how to run the business.' He glanced over at Rita. 'Is that a fair statement?'

'Sure,' she said, 'but that doesn't make my husband a killer. Sonny is far more reasonable than Bart ever was. My brother was always looking for short cuts. You know, the easy way. Fast money. Easy money. Sonny is different. He believes in an honest day's pay for an honest day's work.'

'Bart preferred bribes and threats, did he?'

'Bart wasn't a business man, if that's what you mean.'

'What sort of man was he, Rita?' asked Wallace, in a softer voice. 'Why would someone want to kill your brother?'

'Oh, I don't know,' said Rita. 'Bart was a bully, y'know? He'd use his muscle a bit. If he couldn't make you see it his way, he had a man who could.'

'Does that sort of behaviour fly in the construction business?' said Reyes. 'If Bart's pushing people around, why not go to the cops and report it?'

Rita put her head back and let out a shrill laugh. 'The cops?'

Wallace glanced across at Reyes.

'What's so funny?' said Reyes. 'You don't have much faith in the LAPD?'

'It's not that,' said Rita.

'Care to elaborate?' said Wallace. Her face hardened. 'You do want to find out who put a bullet in Bart's brain, don't you?'

Rita fondled the cup, staring at it as though it were a crystal ball.

'It was probably Bart BS-ing, trying to impress people, but, well – he said he owned a cop.'

'Your brother was bribing a cop? Did he tell you his name?'

'No. I mean, I don't think he did.'

'Does the name Raymond Brooks, or Ray, ring any bells?' asked Reyes. Wallace shot him a look like thunder.

'No.'

'Does the name Cresner sound familiar?' Wallace said.

'Cresner? Yes. That's the cop Bart was accused of shooting.'

'Yes.'

'I don't know if that's who Bart was bribing. All I know for sure is that that my brother was scared of this cop too.'

'So, you do know about some of your brother's dirty dealings,' Wallace said.

Rita lifted the cup to her lips, as though she was going to take a sip, then changed her mind, put it down quickly.

'Tell us what you know about the shooting of Detective Cresner,' said Reyes. 'Don't make me charge you with obstruction of justice.'

The worry on her face deepened. She tapped the cup on the table. 'I found out all of this after the fact, after the shooting. If I tell you...'

'If you know anything, now is the time to tell it.'

'Bart told me that he had gone to make a drug buy. He found his dealer in his usual spot. Unfortunately, Cresner was already there. He said it looked like Cresner was shaking the pusher down. One thing led to another. Bart said Cresner threw the dealer aside and reached for his gun. Bart swore that he shot him in self-defense. But Cresner's a cop, so no one believed him.'

'Do you know the dealer's name?' Wallace asked.

'No. I didn't approve of Bart's drug use. I tried to distance myself from it. Like I said, I didn't find out most of this until after the shooting and Bart's arrest.'

'Do you know who was supplying drugs to your brother in jail?'

She took a deep breath and slowly exhaled. 'I didn't know he was getting drugs in jail. I was hoping that being locked up, he could get clean.'

'Have you ever heard of someone named Duke? Dwayne Duke maybe? Wallace asked.

Rita Giordano shook her head. 'No. Sorry.'

'How about Arsenio Ignatiez?' Reyes asked. 'No.'

'Do you know anyone who might have wanted to harm your brother?'

'I'm sure there were a lot of people, but I don't know who they are.' Rita shifted her gaze to Reyes. 'Maybe it was that cop my brother was afraid of.'

'A logical choice. Instead of gamblers and drug dealers, we'll focus on a cop we're not even sure exists,' Reyes said. 'One last question, Mrs Giordano.' *And one more bluff on my part.* 'We already know why your husband wanted your brother out of the way, but do you know of any reason why your husband would want Mr Simons dead?'

There was a pause. Rita appeared confused, then she gasped. 'Oh, no. No. My husband wouldn't hurt anybody.'

'Okay. If that's the way you want to play it,' Reyes said, 'Let me put it another way. Do you want to take this opportunity to tell us your version of what happened to your brother and Mr Simons? If so, now is the time.'

'I don't have a version.' She began picking at the cup again.

Leaving Rita to ponder what was happening, Wallace and Reyes returned to IR One. This time there were no pleasantries. Wallace started speaking before she sat down.

'Sonny, were you surprised to hear your brother-in-law had been murdered?'

'Honestly? It didn't surprise me that someone capped his ass. Bart was riding the pale horse. It had to catch up with him eventually.'

'The thing is, Sonny,' said Wallace, 'we know you're lying to us. Rita's been very informative about the business. You were happy to let Bart deal with Simons, until Bart got dead, of course. Then you contacted Simons for dinner, just to keep everything on an even keel, yes?'

'You don't know what you're talking about,' Giordano sneered.

'If only Bart hadn't mucked up and shot a cop. You don't do drugs, do you, Sonny?'

'No,' said Giordano.

'Of course you don't. I guess you don't do anything wrong at all. The only honest

175

builder in LA, huh?'

Giordano lost his smile.

'Sonny,' interrupted Reyes. 'We've got you on the bribes. We'll pull the banking records, charge you and your wife with aiding fraud, and no one this side of Korea Town will do business with you when you eventually get out.'

'I've told you. My wife had nothing to do with any of this.'

Wallace let silence fall for twenty seconds.

'Look,' said Giordano. 'I've given you everything I can. I want to know who killed Bart as much as you do.'

'Do you know the name of the cop who was looking after him?'

The color rushed from Giordano's face.

'We know that Bart was in with a dirty cop, Sonny. Were you in, too?'

'Rita told you this?'

'Rita said he was scared of the cop.'

'How do I know you two aren't dirty, too?'

'So there is a cop?'

Another long silence. 'Look, if I tell you what I know, will you leave Rita out of this?'

'Tell us, and we'll see what we can do.'

Giordano took a deep breath. 'Bart came by the morning before he was killed.'

Reyes tried to keep his face from displaying any emotion. *Now we're getting somewhere.*

'What time?' asked Wallace.

'Mid-morning. Maybe eleven-ish.'

'What did he say?'

'He said somebody was following him. There were times Bart made up shit to make himself sound more important, more exciting, but I think he was telling the truth that day.'

'Why? What happened?'

'He looked scared to death. He kept looking out the windows, checking the street.'

'Did he say who it was?'

'No. He said that if the guy knew he was there, Rita's and my life wouldn't be worth a plug nickel.'

'Did he say who this guy was?'

'He said his name was Duke.'

'Dwayne Duke?'

Giordano looked at them both with furtive eyes. 'I don't know. Just Duke. Bart said he was going to lie low in a motel for a few days over in Glendale. Figure out what to do. Then Bart said to forget what he had said.'

'Why do you think he said that?' Reyes asked.

'I think he was afraid that the person following him might somehow find him, so he didn't want anyone to know where he was.'

'So his plans were to hide out in LA. He wasn't going to head out of town or something?'

'I don't know. He had some clothes in a bag, but he needed cash. I gave him about four hundred bucks. He said if we needed to reach him, to use the cell. He didn't want us to know exactly where he was. If anyone showed up, we were supposed to play dumb. Then he took off and we never saw him again.'

'What kind of car was he driving?'

'We lent him my wife's car. We took his and parked it in our garage.'

'What kind of car did you give him?'

'A 2005 Jeep Wrangler. Silver.'

'And where is this vehicle now?'

'I have no clue,' said Giordano. 'We never saw Bart again.'

'License?'

'California plate, DFW62 I.'

Wallace scribbled on the paper in front of her. 'We're going to have to check a few of these things out. We'll need to hold you until we do that.'

'Aw, for the love...'

'We'll have an officer escort your wife back to your house. We need to tow Pearl's car to our impound lot. You don't have a problem with that, do you?'

'Who gives a shit?'

'We'll check this information as quickly as we can.'

Giordano threw his hand forward in disgust. Wallace and Reyes left the room and closed the door.

Wallace looked at the notes. 'Let me give the description of Mrs Giordano's car to a

178

patrol. They can check the motels in that area. Of course, considering the records most motels keep, Pearl could have signed in dressed as Groucho Marx, or said he was driving a pink Studebaker and the desk clerk wouldn't have batted an eye.'

'He'd have to give a credit card to register.'

Wallace looked at Reyes as though he had suddenly grown a tail. 'Pearl bribed city officials, used drugs, shot a cop and you don't think he might have a phony ID or credit card?'

'You know what I think?'

'Tell me.'

'I think we should go get a sandwich. That cookie didn't do it for me.'

17

Kahn had been running with Wagner for over five years, and he knew his partner couldn't pass a mirror without admiring his own reflection. So it was pleasing to see him now, transfixed in the Precinct changing-rooms. Camouflage pants. Sandals. A bright yellow, form-fitting T-shirt. Moussed hair.

'All we can hope for,' Mangan said, 'is that it gets very dark, very early – and I'm talking inside an elephant's ass dark – or that the johns are blind and desperate.'

'That's not really helping,' Wagner said, as he continued to stare in the mirror. 'But I'll be honest. Even I wouldn't fuck me.'

'You might want to add a few more crunches to your exercise routine,' Mangan said. 'Getting a little loose in the abs.'

'Yeah, that's good. It really makes me want to get out there and strut my stuff.'

'If you shave your chest, we can change that shirt for a net.'

Wagner turned and looked at Mangan. 'Whoever writes your material is overpaid, captain.'

'I never kid,' Mangan said. He grabbed Wagner's arm. 'Jesus, look at the size of that bruise.'

'Ow. Hey. That's where that kid clobbered me with a flower-pot.'

'Have somebody put some makeup over that. Johns don't want their tarts all beat up.'

Krajcek wired Wagner up. A GPS unit about the size of a dime was affixed to his belt-buckle for electronic tracking. He was given an iPod which had been modified to work as a walkie talkie. The earphones allowed Wagner to hear the conversation from the police observers and there was actually a mic housed behind the dial.

'We're ready,' Krajcek said. 'Okay, everybody, let's get down to the Sepulveda Corridor. We'll check out a few spots in the light before we pick our fishing hole.'

Wagner looked at Kahn. 'How did we decide that I should be the gay guy and you get to be the cop in the car?'

In his best Schwarzenegger imitation, Kahn puffed his chest up and said 'Captain Mangan said he wanted a girlie man.'

'Remind me when we get back to beat the shit out of you.'

'Will do,' Kahn laughed. 'Tell you what. When we're done, I'll buy you a drink.'

'I'm not that kind of guy.'

Krajcek led the way to the underground police parking lot where he picked up the car they called the 'pimp-mobile'. It was a beat-up black low-rider with heavily-tinted windows. The whole idea was that it blended in and nobody in their right mind would want to steal it. In the corridor, it would fit right in. As they pulled out into another Hollywood evening, Krajcek said, 'I know the captain gave you a short briefing on our operations, but seriously, "Stand there looking cute until some guy wants to fuck your ass and then arrest him," is kind of a simplified description of what we do and how we do it.'

'I thought so,' Kahn said. 'You want Wagner to kind of walk the walk and wiggle his ass all over the place, right?'

'Have either of you worked the street before?'

'I can't speak for what Wagner does after

hours, but I'm new to this.'

'Having a good time tonight, are you?' Wagner said.

'So far.'

'I'll do a slow cruise down Sepulveda,' Krajcek said, 'and try to spot an area where there is some early activity but not too much. We'll avoid the areas where the women are working. We're looking for different clientele.'

A light drizzle began to fall. Krajcek turned on the wipers. They drove through the neighborhood for thirty minutes checking likely stretches off the main drag.

'I think we'll go back a few blocks. The boys who are there are pretty popular. They'll be gone quickly, but while they're on display they'll help draw in the lookers.'

'So, Wagner is sloppy seconds,' Kahn said.

'Jesus criminy,' Wagner said. 'I'm glad I'm getting out of the car pretty soon.'

Krajcek pulled into a parking lot down Haynes Street, a block off of Sepulveda. He reminded Wagner of the rest of the process, and tested the mic and headphones. 'We'll be right around the corner from you. As soon as the offer is made, Kahn and I will pull up and make the arrest. We have several patrols on notice to help us shuttle the johns in for booking.'

'Okay, let me out.'

'Wait,' Krajcek said. 'I'm as serious as a heart attack now. You are not, under any

182

circumstances, to get into a car with one of the punters. If you do find yourself in some kind of trouble, the code word is "appetite". You have all of that?'

'Sure.'

'I know you think that you're a cop and can kick the crap out of any of those fairies out there if they try anything. I have to tell you, some of the guys that come around here are pretty damn tough. Some are armed.'

'Yeah, yeah. Tough. Stay out of cars. Appetite.'

'Go ahead,' Krajcek said. 'We'll see you soon.'

Wagner climbed out of the back seat and headed toward Sepulveda. Krajcek did a U-turn, slowly bringing the pimp mobile back onto Haynes Street and within fifty feet of where Wagner was standing.

'Now, we wait,' Krajcek said. But the wait was only seconds long. 'What the hell is he doing?'

Wagner was singing.

'*Well, she's all geared up, Walkin' down the street...*'

'Is that Guns'n'Roses?' said Krajcek. 'God, what an awful voice.'

'You see what I have to put up with,' said Kahn.

'Hey, Wagner,' Krajcek muttered into his mic. 'Keep it down, will ya? This tape can be admitted as evidence; we don't want the judge throwing it out for offending his musical taste.'

'You got any requests?' asked Harlen.

'Yeah, shuddup,' Kahn replied.

'Hey guys, there's a car coming.'

The sound of an engine came through the radio speaker, then died.

'Hey, you're new here,' said a man's voice.

'Yeah. You can be the first.'

Kahn smothered a laugh. 'He's got to be ready to puke.'

'First ever?' the john asked. 'Or the first tonight?'

'Let's say I'm new in town and leave it at that.'

'Don't be so damn shy. Come closer. Let me get a look at what you're selling.'

Wagner must have leaned in, because when the john spoke again his voice was louder, almost like he was sitting in the back seat.

'Get in. We'll go up the road a bit.'

'What did you have in mind?'

'Come on, hop in.'

'Sure,' Wagner said. The sound of the car door slamming was followed by the sound of the engine.

'Shit!' Krajcek said. 'I told him not to get in the fucking cars.'

'Come on, move.' Kahn said.

They listened as Wagner continued to entice the john to make an offer for sex, but the old man was cagey. He had obviously played the game before. Finally, the words they were waiting to hear crackled through their radio.

'All right, how much for a blowjob?'

'Twenty bucks.'

'Done and done. How about right up there?'

'Perfect. Is that Pierce Street?'

'Come on,' Kahn said. 'That's a block away.'

Krajcek stomped the pedal and the car screeched away from the sidewalk. He rode the brakes as he whipped the wheel in a U-turn, then lunged forward toward the corner of Haynes and Pierce.

'I don't see them,' Kahn said. 'What happened to the mic?'

'There they are,' Krajcek pointed down the street about a block. He slowed and rolled up behind a dark-red Taurus.

'I should have known,' Kahn said.

Wagner had the john spread-eagled, face-down on the hood.

Krajcek called for a shuttle. Kahn walked over and checked the perpetrator. 'You all right there?'

'I want to report an assault,' he said. 'This man claims he is a cop. He forced me to drive him down here and...'

'This is Vaughn Green,' Wagner handed the man's wallet to Kahn. 'Vaughn, this is my

185

partner, Detective Kahn. He was kind enough to record everything you said. Now shut the fuck up until your ride gets here.'

'No problems?' Kahn asked.

'Piece of cake,' Wagner said. 'Isn't that right Vaughn?'

Green groaned. 'Can I at least get off the hood? It kind of hurts.'

'You don't like being bent over?' Wagner took his arm and helped him down. 'Let's sit you down over here in the grass.' He walked Green across the sidewalk to a thin strip of grass and tugged on him hard. Green landed on his ass with a thump.

'Ouch. Damn it, you're too rough.'

'I'm guessing wrong a lot with you, aren't I?' Wagner lit a cigarette and joined Kahn and Krajcek by the car.

'Not so bad for the first time,' Krajcek said. 'But you were told not to get in the car.'

'I sized him up and figured he wasn't a threat.'

'Uh-huh,' Krajcek said. 'Stay out of the cars. Got it?'

'You're the boss.'

A prison van rolled up a few minutes later. 'The shuttle is here, Mr Green.' Krajcek walked over to the prisoner. 'Time for you to take another ride. Your car will be towed to an impound lot. They'll explain all of that downtown.' He escorted Green to the patrol car and handed him over to the uniforms.

'See you soon, I'm sure.'

He joined Wagner and Kahn. 'That's the way it's supposed to work, minus the getting in the car part.'

'Well then, so far so good,' Kahn said. 'I'm ready.'

'Me, too,' Wagner said. 'I didn't mind the take down, but I'm going to tell you that it is downright humiliating to be standing on a corner like that.'

'I know,' Krajcek said. 'But you only have to do it for a few hours. The real prostitutes are out here every night. It's an occupation born out of desperation in most cases. Worst of all are the kids that are out here. We try to round them up, get them to a service agency. Most of them are back on the street in a few days.'

Wagner threw his half-finished cigarette to the damp street and crushed it under his shoe. 'Yeah, well. Maybe we should get back to work.'

Kahn and Krajcek climbed into their car as Wagner took his place back on the sidewalk beneath a streetlamp.

'Hey, buddy,' said Kahn into the mic. 'Did you say only twenty bucks for a blowjob?'

'Thirty to you, asshole.'

18

'The patrol found the jeep at the Pine Tree Motel off West Sunset,' Reyes said. 'Want to head over and check it out?'

Wallace was standing with her back to him at the fax machine, leafing through a set of sheets, while Albanese sucked on a bottle of water. 'Just a minute, Sal. This looks interesting.'

Reyes grabbed his Coke, walked up beside his partner. 'Whatcha got?'

'Hackett's come good, Sal. These are Simons' medical records.'

Reyes couldn't help but notice that the top sheet said *Confined to FID personnel.*

'Should we be looking at these?'

'The Doc must have dialed the last digit wrong on the number,' she said. 'FID are using the fax in the old squad room.'

'I've never known Hackett to get shit like that wrong,' said Albanese. 'The guy's slow as hell, but he's as precise as they come.'

Wallace smiled, and arched an eyebrow. 'I think we can both thank him for this *professional oversight.*'

'Good old Hackett,' said Reyes. 'At least not everyone's bending over for FID.

Anything interesting?'

'He's been receiving psychiatric treatment since 1992, paid for by the military. Depression brought on by Post-Traumatic Stress Syndrome.'

'That fits with the suicide angle.'

'Combine depression with the booze and pills we found, it makes sense.'

'This is interesting. It says Simons probably died between six and eight in the morning.'

'That's earlier than we thought,' said Reyes. 'What are they basing that on?'

'Body temp and lividity,' said Wallace. 'Simons died from a 9x18 Makarov bullet to the right temple, same gun as used in the killing of Bartholomew Pearl. I owe you twenty bucks, but under the circumstances I don't give a shit. Everything's there. Simons knew that Pearl had probably squealed to get released. Murder for revenge – suicide exacerbated by mental health problems.'

'Hell, for twenty bucks, I'll even volunteer to type this one up,' said Reyes. 'Leave the dirty cop witch-hunt to FID.'

'You think it's Cresner?' said Albanese.

'If he's involved, he's not the cop Pearl was afraid of,' said Wallace. 'The guy can hardly walk, let alone chase down a guy like Pearl.'

'Well, it sure as hell ain't Brooks,' said Reyes. 'Ray couldn't scare a five-year-old child.'

Wallace glared at him. They hadn't mentioned the intel from the jail, and Reyes knew that Wallace wanted to keep it under wraps for now.

Albanese coughed, and Wallace was looking at him strangely. *Shit.*

He turned round to see Brooks standing behind him. 'Hey, Sergeant.'

'It's good to know I inspire such confidence in the squad.'

'I didn't mean it like that...'

'Save it. I know what you meant, Detective Reyes. Your jeep's been located, hasn't it?'

'It has,' he replied. 'We were just heading out.'

'Better go then, hadn't you?'

Reyes struggled to find the right words, and Wallace came to his rescue.

'We sure had. Come on, Sal.'

She half-pushed him out of the doors.

Reyes didn't speak again until they were driving near to their destination. 'I was trying to stick up for the guy. I don't think he's got anything to do with it.'

'Ray'll get over it – he's just a little sensitive at the moment.'

A green neon sign in the shape of a pine tree signaled they'd reached the Pine Tree Motel. Another in pink said there were Vacancies. Wallace steered off the road. Off to the left side of the parking lot sat a squad car, with two uniforms in the front seat. The silver Jeep Wrangler was alongside, and she pulled up behind it.

Reyes walked over to the open window of the squad car, leaving Phil to call in their location. Tina Lantz was sitting in the driver's seat, with her legs out of the door and Tibor Martin was leaning his rangy frame up on the bonnet. 'How's it going?'

'All right. We thought maybe you had forgotten about us.'

'Have you spoken with the motel manager?'

'I've told him we're out here,' Lantz said.

'Let's open this baby up,' said Reyes.

'I've got my kit on the hood,' Martin said. They walked over to the front of the Jeep and Martin inserted a Slim Jim down the side of the driver's door window. He wriggled with it for a few seconds.

'Manufacturer's security.'

Instead, he selected a latch hook and slipped it through the tight space between the window and the molding. With the deft moves of a pro, he latched the door handle and gave it a quick tug. The lock released. He opened the door and pressed the unlock button. 'There ya go.'

Wallace climbed into the front seat while Reyes opened the back door, quickly determined there was nothing of interest and moved to the back of the car and opened the hatch. He rummaged through the side pockets and checked around the spare tire.

'It looks to me like he picked this baby up from the Giordanos and drove straight over here. There's not an empty cup or food wrapper back here,' Reyes said. 'Anything up front?'

'Nothing,' Wallace said.

'Let's go talk to the desk clerk.'

Reyes stepped into the small, dingy lobby. The low-wattage lighting did little to hide the fact that everything was old and cheap. The clerk was a young, black, female dressed in the uniform of the Pine Tree Motel, a green vest, white blouse and black skirt. Her name tag read LaQuisha. The round pin she wore said *Ask About FGP!*

'Can I help you?' she asked.

'I'm Detective Reyes. My partner...' he turned to look for Phil. She stepped in with a photo in hand '...is Detective Wallace. We were wondering if you might recognize this man.'

Wallace laid the four by five photo of Pearl on the counter.

'No. I've never seen him.'

'We're pretty sure that he stayed here. Probably checked in yesterday before two in the afternoon.'

'Excuse me? If I didn't see him, telling me what time he came by is not going to help.'

'Is your manager here?' Wallace asked.

'You can talk to him all you want but it won't make the man appear where he ain't.'

LaQuisha picked up the phone and pushed a button. 'Mr Mandusco. This is LaQuisha. Could you come to the front desk, please? The police want to see you. Mm-hmmm.' She smiled at the detectives. 'He'll be right out.'

Mr Mandusco came scurrying out of the office to the front desk.

'Wallace and Reyes, LAPD,' said Wallace. 'We were curious if you saw this man yesterday. We believe he was a guest. Your employee said she hasn't seen him but his car is in your parking lot.'

Mandusco frowned at LaQuisha. 'I recognize him, officer. I can't recall his name off the top of my head but I remember he was very picky about which room he wanted. It had to be in back. Ground floor. I gave him room...' he punched a few keys, '...eighteen. Yes. Clement Rosen. Room eighteen.'

'Clement Rosen? Is that the name he used?'

'Yes.'

'You're sure it's this man?' Wallace asked, pointing at the photo of Bart Pearl.

'Absolutely. He had a credit card – we require one even if you pay cash, like he did.' He opened a drawer and pulled out a small gray box. Inside were alphabet dividers. He flipped the R tab, reached behind it and pulled out a charge-card slip.

'I'd like to take this credit card receipt, please,' Wallace said. 'You'll get it back.'

'Fine,' Mandusco said, and handed it over. He loosened his tie and undid the top button on his shirt. 'Is there a problem? We don't want any trouble.'

'You're fine,' Wallace said. 'Mr Rosen, whose real name was Bartholomew Pearl, isn't doing so well. He's dead.'

'Oh God.' There was a look of panic on his face. 'Here? Is he in my motel?'

'Easy, friend,' Reyes said. 'He's not here, but we do need to take a look in his room if you could give us the key.'

'I'll get it,' LaQuisha said. She pulled out a plastic key card and programmed it.

'Can you tell us anything about Pearl? Did he say or do anything unusual? Maybe ask you to put something in the safe perhaps?'

'He left a Do Not Disturb request,' Mandusco said. 'He didn't want to be disturbed for anything and that included maid service. No cleaning, no nothing.'

LaQuisha handed Wallace the key card to room eighteen. 'Well, thank you all. You've been most helpful. The police impound lot will be sending a tow-truck to remove Mr Pearl's Jeep Wrangler. Um, if he had a room in back, why did he park over on the side?'

'We're having the parking lot re-paved. They're working in the back right now. Guests have to walk through.'

Reyes was first out of the lobby. He held the door for Wallace, who was already on the phone to the station. 'Hey, this is Philippa. Could you check and see if a Clement Rosen reported a stolen credit card? No rush. Leave me a note at the station.'

'According to the receipt, check-in was at six minutes after twelve,' Wallace said. 'Yesterday's timeline has been fairly tight. Around ten at his apartment. Around eleven at Giordano's. Here at noon. Dead by early afternoon.'

Together with Lantz and Martin, they made their way around to the rear of the building.

'Pearl came here to hide,' said Reyes. 'He was going deep, low and out of sight, even covering his tracks by swapping cars. Hell, he didn't even want the maid coming in. Sounds to me like he was pretty damned scared. So, who would he break cover for to go out and see? Whoever it was, was probably his killer.' Reyes ran the card LaQuisha had given him through the electronic lock. A green light flashed. He pushed the door open.

'Déjà-fucking-vu.' They stared into the room, which had been turned upside down. Reyes reached around the corner and flipped the light switch.

Drawers, a straight-back chair, both mattresses, pillows, clothes, paintings, the telephone and even the Gideon bible had been hurled into the center of the room. On top of the small mountain was a laundry cart.

'This guy needs maid service,' said Martin.

Wallace turned to the uniforms. 'Tina, you seal off this room. Tibor, get CSI down here, too.'

Wallace and Reyes pulled on pairs of latex gloves. Reyes moved to the left, Wallace to the right.

Reyes picked his way over the carpet to the far side of the pile of debris. A large red stain covered the side of the laundry cart.

'Phil, I got some blood over here.'

At the back of the room was a large mirror with a two-sink counter. A door to the left opened to the bathroom. The door to the right was closed.

Dark stains in the carpet in front of the sink were nearly perfect circles, suggesting somebody was there for several minutes bleeding, but not moving. Wallace looked back toward the cart, then at Reyes. She signaled for quiet, then pointed to the door on the right. She and Reyes pulled out their guns. Reyes nodded. Wallace grasped the knob. She turned it slowly, then with a push, shoved it open.

It was empty.

'Whew,' Wallace said. 'Look at the mess in here.' She turned on the lights. The shower curtain was gone. Large smears of blood stained the bottom and sides of the tub. There was a red puddle around the drain.

Blood spatters reached a foot above the tub.

'Pearl didn't go out to see anyone.' Reyes gestured toward the tub. 'I'll let the crime scene boys give us an official guess, but I think it ended right here. The shooter let him drain and then probably wrapped him in the shower curtain.'

'Pearl obviously had a pint left in him when he was put in the laundry basket.'

'Our killer apparently got a little sloppy putting the body in the cart. The curtain must have slipped or filled with blood and leaked out, soaking the bottom corner. Even so, the cart remained good cover to move the body. Unless you were right on top of him, it would look like someone was hauling dirty laundry.'

'So he loads the body in a truck or car trunk,' said Wallace, 'then puts the cart back inside so it won't be discovered. He takes Pearl's body to the Green Cheese building and starts the fire. Pearl didn't know it, but by requesting he not be bothered, he gave his killer time to get away.'

'Remember how Giordano said Pearl thought he was being followed? I'm going to take a guess that he wasn't being paranoid.'

Reyes nodded. 'This was an execution. One shot to the head.'

'Remind you of anything?'

Reyes looked at her without speaking for a few seconds.

'You don't think Simons killed himself, do you?'

'Come on, Sal. It's exactly the same, isn't it? And again, no one heard the shot.'

'Someone else is pulling the trigger. This cop?'

'I'm not sure, but I think we need to have a patrol at Giordano's house. In fact, we need to put a guard on Giordano at the station.'

'At the station? What the hell for?'

'Pearl said that if the guy that followed him found out that he had visited the Giordanos, their lives might not be worth a damn.'

'Okay, I understand protecting Rita, but don't you think Sonny is pretty safe? I mean, he is surrounded by a dozen cops.'

'Yeah, a dozen good cops,' Wallace said. 'And maybe one very bad one.'

19

Reyes and Wallace waited until Drake finished photographing the bloodied furniture and the rest of the scene, then worked alongside Withingham's CSI team as they rummaged through Pearl's motel room. Forensics dabbed at the blood stains. Each item was inspected, checked for fingerprints and trace evidence and then returned to its proper place, if possible.

'Hey, Sal,' Wallace said, 'do you think whoever did this found what they were looking for?'

'Who knows,' Sal replied. 'From the spatter, I'd say Pearl was on his knees when he was shot, which suggests that he had at least some dialogue with his killer before the bullet did its work. Perhaps the gunman wanted to know where this thing was.'

'But he didn't tell him?'

'Perhaps it wasn't ever even here,' said Reyes. 'Hell, we don't even know what we're looking for.'

Withingham laughed. 'Molly. Jason. You see why you're better off in CSI? Detectives tend to get a little unbalanced.'

Reyes' eyes wandered through the room for maybe the tenth time. *Looked in there. Opened that. Checked that.* His eyes caught the corner of the Gideon bible protruding from under the sheets.

Reyes picked it up and thumbed through it. A small, square item flew from between the pages. 'Hey!' Reyes said. 'I found something.' He laid the bible down on the bureau and picked up the little foil pack. 'Jesus. Some sick puppy put a condom in the bible.'

'I think I can say without fear of contradiction that whoever killed Pearl wasn't looking for a rubber,' Wallace said.

'It's a glow-in-the-dark model. Someone

199

check that for fingerprints.'

Reyes checked the bathroom next, behind the tank, in the tank, and in the rolls of toilet paper, including the two spares which had been unwrapped, probably by the intruder, and thrown on the floor. The suspect had apparently looked inside each but Reyes wondered if maybe the hidden item was between the sheets. He began unrolling the first roll.

Wallace walked over to the bath-tub.

'Forensics looked in the drain,' said Reyes.

Wallace reached up and took off the shower head, and began unscrewing. She looked inside, then set the shower head on the edge of the tub.

'Well, I suppose we could take the drain off the sink, but I can't believe Pearl brought a pipe wrench with him.' Wallace stopped in the middle of the room. 'You know, I wonder...'

'What? You have something, partner?'

'We made a couple of assumptions. Maybe they're backward.'

'I'm listening.'

'We've been assuming Pearl had an enemy and that person killed him. But, what if Pearl had something our suspect wanted bad enough to kill him for it? We know the killer tore the hell out of several places looking for something.'

Reyes cocked his head slightly. 'Okay, but we still don't know if he found it.'

Wallace smiled and shook her head. 'He didn't find it here. Think about it. Pearl's apartment was ransacked *after* this place, if we believe Mr and Mrs Scrabble. Pearl must have gone home first to get this item, and brought it here.'

'Or it was at Giordano's place all along,' said Reyes. 'Maybe Pearl picked it up along with the cash and the Jeep.'

'It may have been the only hope he had of staying alive.'

'So why didn't he give it to his killer?'

'Perhaps he said it was in the apartment. If he knew that this thing was all that was keeping him alive, handing it right over would have been like signing his own death warrant.'

'Whatever it is must not be too big, then. The killer tore apart mattresses but he also looked through books – which is why they were scattered around the apartment. The paintings were checked, too, so the thing must be slim, not too large, not too bulky. So, where haven't we looked?' Reyes asked.

Wallace's eyes did a tour of the room, then she snapped her fingers. 'The shower curtain rod. It's hollow.' Reyes carefully stepped into the bloody bathroom and unscrewed the rod. It was hollow – and empty. He shook his head.

'Damn it,' said Wallace.

Reyes stood in front of the sink. To his left

was the open clothes rack. On the opposite wall was a bracket where the complimentary iron and ironing board should be. Pearl's killer had checked those and they now lay in the pile. Reyes eyes widened as he realized the coat rack was made from hollow metal tubes, just like the shower curtain. He dug in his pocket, took out his utility knife and popped out the screwdriver blade.

Wallace moved closer. She held the rack as Reyes began unscrewing the chrome tubes. He quickly removed the three screws on one end, moved around Wallace to the other end and removed the remaining screws. As soon as Reyes had the first tube, he held it up like a telescope and looked toward the light over the sink.

'Bingo.' He jammed his finger into the tiny tube but couldn't reach the item inside.

'Let me have it,' Wallace said. She rapped it on the floor several times until the item inside slid out a quarter of an inch. 'Got it.'

A piece of thin card had been rolled tight and then taped. Reyes handed Wallace his knife and she snipped the tape. The card unrolled, revealing two photos. Wallace stared at the first for a few seconds. 'Holy shit.'

She handed it to Reyes.

A black-and-white image, showing a middle-aged man sitting on the edge of the bed. He was leaning backward on his arms. Kneeling on the floor in front of him, performing oral sex, was a younger man. 'Holy shit,' Reyes repeated. 'That's Sam Davey.'

'That it is,' said Wallace. She handed the second to Reyes. It was similar to the first, but this time the owner of Sphinx Construction had a hand on the back of the other man's head. His face suggested that the encounter was reaching its climax.

'The first question is,' said Wallace, 'who's the dude on the action end of his dong?'

'Let's check the other two tubes.'

Reyes swiftly undid the screws that held the remaining tubes in place. Each contained more photos. 'It's the freakin' mother lode.'

'Sounds like good news,' Withingham said. 'We're done, but do you want those tubes dusted as well?'

'Doesn't look like the killer found them,' said Reyes. 'But see if you can get a match on Pearl.'

After all of the different teams had departed, Wallace took another look at the photos. 'I wonder if we can figure out where these were taken,' she asked Reyes.

'I'd like to know who took them,' Reyes replied. 'This looks like blackmail. You remember how Davey was so keen to shut his wife up about the City Council?'

'These make a damn fine motive to kill Pearl.'

'The photos sure as hell explain the frantic searches.'

'I think we should talk to Mr Davey again. He might like to see these – or not.'

'Do you want to run out to his house again or have him come in?'

'Oh, he's coming in – in cuffs. I'm going to call Siley and ask him to have someone pick him up. I think we've seriously underestimated Mr Davey.'

20

Wagner checked his reflection in the car window. Kahn was beginning to think he liked his new look. 'Is it me or am I doing all the work? It's not enough that I have to lure them in, I have to nail them as well.'

'If you'd follow procedure,' Krajcek said, 'you wouldn't be getting your cool outfit all wrinkled.'

'Try to move in a little faster next time.'

'You don't have any patience,' said Krajcek. 'We launch the second we hear a financial arrangement agreed to. You say "twenty bucks" for a hummer and as soon as he nods, you cuff the guy yourself. We can't hear a nod you know.'

'How much longer do I have to do this? It's a pain in the ass.'

'It's only a pain in the ass if you go through with it,' Kahn said.

'Jesus. What's with you? You've been throwing out one-liners all night.'

'What can I say?'

'Nothing would be good.' Wagner walked back to the corner. He whispered into the iPod mic. 'A new shift has arrived. Jeez, I'm starting to look like the Queen of the Corner now. We're talking butt-ugly competition.'

'Some of the old pros have regulars,' Krajcek said. 'They stand in front of a hotel and go straight up to a room when one of their johns comes by. If enough regulars come, they don't have to do corner work.'

'Got it.'

A thunderous bang hit the car. 'What the fuck was that?' Kahn yelled. He turned to his right as he reached for his weapon. Krajcek spun as well. A man bent over and grinned at the officers through the door window.

'Captain?' Krajcek said.

Captain Mangan leaned in, his arms resting on Kahn's door. 'Easy guys. Looks like you boys are a bit complacent. Wagner may be out there peddling his ass but you need to be alert. If some hopped-up motherfucker comes looking for an easy mark, you're gonna catch one in the back of the skull.'

Krajcek put both hands on the wheel and exhaled. 'That could have gotten you killed as well, Captain.'

'Know your enemy,' Mangan said, grinning. 'So, how many johns have we surprised tonight with the offer of free room and board?'

'Kind of slow. Three were sent down. One scared off.'

'He figured it was a set up?'

'I don't know if he thought Wagner was a cop or simply sensed something wasn't right, but for no apparent reason, he cut out.'

'I think he got a look at Wagner in the light,' Kahn said.

Mangan nodded. 'It happens. You can never tell about some people. It's a little after seven, so in roughly another hour it'll be dark. That's when the trolls arrive.'

'Wagner said the regulars were gathering in front of the Biscayne,' said Krajcek.

'Really? Too bad. They'll lure some trade away from us.' He stood up and checked the street. 'Tell you what, if things don't pick up by eight, we'll call it a night. How about I get you guys some coffee?'

'Sounds good,' Krajcek said. 'Two sugars.'

'Black,' Kahn said.

'I'll be back in a few minutes.'

Kahn watched Mangan walk off in the rear-view mirror. Wagner was humming to himself again.

'You follow any sports besides the NFL?' Krajcek asked.

'The Dodgers. College football.'

'How about the NBA?'

'Nah.'

Kahn glanced in the mirror. The sidewalk was empty. He was determined to spot Mangan when he came back. Being caught off guard like that bothered him. It was the kind of thing Angie always warned him about. Getting too relaxed in a dangerous job. The radio suddenly screeched. 'Appetite! Ouch, shit … appetite you fuckin' assholes.'

Kahn was out and running. He could hear the muted shuffling of a fight now even without the radio. As he reached the corner he could see three young men pounding the snot out of Wagner. He was flat on his back, his legs propped up against the two foot high concrete wall. The assault had cleared the corner. No one had stayed to lend a hand. They had simply vanished into the night.

'Fucking fag,' shouted one of the muggers, wearing a UCLA jacket. 'Get your AIDS infected ass out of here.'

Kahn hopped the wall, pulled his weapon. 'Police! Stop and drop.'

The closest thug turned and took a swing at Kahn, who countered with a gun across his jaw. The man spun around and hit the sidewalk. Kahn repeated his order, 'Police!'

The distraction was all Wagner needed. His fist flew up, catching the second man in the groin and dropping him instantly. Wagner rolled and smashed him between the eyes with the back of his fist. 'Bastard!'

The third guy jumped back over the fence to run but Krajcek hit him in the back like a lightning bolt and took him to the sidewalk.

Wagner popped up. He looked at the guy lying on the ground next to him and kicked him in the gut. 'Not so fucking tough when the odds even out, are you punk?'

'What the hell happened?' Krajcek said. He had his member of the trio by the collar, already cuffed.

Wagner gently touched his cheek, then twisted his jaw. 'These three guys came along talking smack. They all looked drunk and I didn't want them screwing things up, so I sat on the wall to let them through.' Wagner brushed off his clothes. 'The one Krajcek is holding punched me right in the forehead. It caught me off guard and toppled me off the wall like fucking Humpty Dumpty. I cracked my head on the pavement.' He touched the back of his head. 'Then all three of the superheroes pounced on me.' Wagner turned and kicked the guy on the ground again. He groaned.

'That's enough,' said Krajcek. He nodded to Kahn. 'I'll get us a wagon.'

Kahn dragged the man he smashed in the mouth closer to the wall and cuffed him. 'What in the hell is the matter with you dumb asses?'

The man spat out some bloody saliva. 'Shit

dude. We were out having a few drinks is all. Then one of the fags tried to pick us up. That one you're standing with. He's the one. We were fuckin' offended, you know?'

'Bad news. The "fag" you decided to assault is an undercover cop. Now, before you say it's his word against the three of you, we recorded everything.'

He looked up at Wagner. 'You're a cop? You sure as hell look queer. Or are you maybe a queer cop?'

Wagner went to kick him like he had the other guy on the ground, but was held back by Kahn. 'Easy, partner.'

A squad car rolled up at the sidewalk, lights flashing. Krajcek leant down.

'I called a wagon.'

'We're not here for you,' said the officer. 'We've got a possible homicide down at the Biscayne.'

Krajcek saw the wagon pull around the corner. 'Here she is.'

The patrol car carried on down the street and disappeared at the next turn.

Kahn and Krajcek loaded the three men into the cage. 'Get them some medical attention,' said Krajcek. 'And find out if they really are college boys. If they are, inform their school's president.'

'The one that's still bent over may not have any balls,' Wagner said. 'Look in his mouth.'

Back at the car, Krajcek's radio beeped.
'Yeah?'

'You boys still on station?' the dispatcher asked.

'Yes. What'dya have?'

'Reported homicide three blocks away. Hotel Biscayne. Want to take a look? I've sent a unit. It should be there any second.'

'They just got here. We'll be right after them.'

'Let's call it a night here,' said Krajcek. 'Harlen's chances of pulling in his current state are practically zero.'

Krajcek dropped Kahn and Wagner at the front steps of the Biscayne, where a bunch of hookers were gathered in small groups with passers-by, business forgotten for the time being.

Wagner grabbed a coat, and walked with Kahn up to the hotel lobby. The paint was peeling off the front of the building, and inside a dirty red carpet led to the clerk's desk.

'What kind of a dive is this?' asked Kahn.

'I'm not sure anyone has spent the night in twenty years,' said Wagner. 'It's a one-sheeter.'

'A one-sheeter?'

'A clean sheet with every fuck.'

'That's disgusting.'

'Beats the hell out of a back alley.'

The clerk was a skinny black guy with two

gold teeth who appeared to drink at least two out of three meals a day.

'Which way to the dead guy?' Wagner said.

'Are you more police?' the clerk asked. His lips tugged hard on a cigarette, despite the regulations.

Kahn had no inclination to stop him. 'Yes.'

'Third floor. Three twelve.'

'Elevator work?'

'The stairs are faster.' He coughed and pointed.

'Great.' Kahn said. 'You the one who found the body?'

'Nah. One of the ... erm ... tenants phoned it in from a payphone. Said he noticed the door was open to the dead guy's room. When he peeked in, he spotted him and notified the front desk.'

'That's you, right?' Krajcek asked.

'That's me. Naturally, I did my civic duty and called the police.'

'But you never went up to see if the man was alive or not?'

'And desert my post?'

The stairs were worn in the center from generations of transients, prostitutes and winos tramping up and down. The place smelled of piss; the second floor especially, as though someone had recently contributed to the odor. The urine smell was accentuated by the yellow-green paint on the walls.

Krajcek opened the door to the third floor.

A light streamed into the hall from an open door. 'Must be the place.'

As they reached three twelve they found two uniforms, one male, one female, standing inside the door, both with smiles on their faces. 'That was quick. To what do we owe this honor?'

'Moreno, Grunwald,' said Krajcek. 'This is Detective Wagner and Kahn. We were working a little vice sting around the corner.'

'Well, that explains him,' Grunwald said nodding toward Wagner. 'The vic is in the bedroom. Cause of death was brain damage.'

'Brain damage?' Kahn asked.

'Yeah, there's a bullet in it. There don't appear to be other wounds but considering the amount of blood, there didn't have to be.' She led them to the bedroom. 'No ID on him, but he's dressed like a streetwalker, so some of the others might be able to put a name on him. Looks to be around twenty to twenty-five years old.'

Kahn looked at the body, sprawled face-down across the bed on the bloodstained sheet. The dead man was fully-clothed. There was one entrance wound in the right side of his head, an exit wound on the other. The spray of blood and brain matter extended from the spot on the bed where he lay to the wall and on the floor in between. It was still sticky.

'He should have known his way around,

how to avoid getting into a bad situation,' Krajcek said.

'Bad luck sucks.' Kahn looked around. The room was dingy and smelled of stale smoke and sex. The place wasn't so dirty that you'd be afraid to use the toilet, but definitely was on the worn-out side of things. At one time the wallpaper was stripes and flowers but they had faded to almost nothing. Several of the wooden floorboards were warped. Both windows had a yellowing shade pulled part of the way down – both crooked. Two straight-back chairs and a battered table sat against the far wall. On top was a metal ashtray which had been emptied but not cleaned.

Wagner leaned in across the body, careful not to touch anything.

'No defensive wounds on either arm, and they took his watch.' He pointed to a narrow pale band around the dead man's right wrist.

'Looks like a straightforward robbery,' said Kahn.

Grunwald had marked one brass casing's spot on the floor with chalk. Kahn checked the dead guy's pockets. Nothing but a lighter.

'Who talked to the desk clerk?' Krajcek asked.

'I did.' Grunwald flipped his note pad open but didn't need the reference. 'Saw nothing. Heard nothing. Couldn't say if this kid was a regular. He came in, paid for the

213

room, took the key and sheets and went upstairs.'

'The clerk didn't see anyone with him?'

'He can't remember.'

'Get the ME to check for sexual activity. There might be a DNA match with his killer.'

As if on cue, Barrett arrived. Three years back, just before he met Angie, Kahn had spent the night with Barrett down at the lab. It was the weirdest place he'd ever got laid. He'd made the mistake of telling Wagner. 'Hi Doc,' Harlen said. 'Many stiff ones down at the morgue?'

'Hello, everyone,' she said, ignoring him. 'Ready to let me do my thing?'

'We're done,' Kahn said. 'I'd appreciate it if you could determine whether the victim had sex recently.'

'Will do,' she said. 'Anything else?'

'Just the usual,' said Kahn, trying to apologise with his eyes for his partner's way with words.

'Give me some space then, gentlemen.'

Kahn, Krajcek and Wagner left the room and walked down the dimly-lit stairs and into the cool air. The lights of two squad cars had cleared the sidewalk of everyone but a couple of drunks laughing wheezily with one another and passing a brown-paper bag between them. Wagner put a cigarette in his mouth.

Mangan was holding a cardboard tray of coffees from Fratelli's, and was speaking with one of the uniforms. When he saw Kahn he shouted over. 'When they told me the lift wasn't working, I thought I'd wait down here. These are gonna be cold...' He looked at Wagner's bruised face. 'What the hell happened to you?'

'Three punk college kids jumped me. For some reason, they thought I was a homo and they didn't apparently care for homos.'

'Trouble seems to love you, detective.' He turned to Kahn and Krajcek, and they each took a coffee. Kahn sipped his: it was indeed cold. 'Well, what do you fellas think happened upstairs?'

'Someone killed themselves a hooker.'

Mangan nodded. 'All right, detective, so what do you think – that we have a new Jack the Ripper on our hands?'

'No,' Kahn said. 'It was just a robbery, I think. Some john didn't feel like paying.'

'And wanted a new watch and cell phone,' added Wagner.

Mangan checked his watch. 'It's a little early, but considering our bait is looking kind of sad, let's call it a night. And anyhow, you guys have a homicide to write up.'

'But we're Vice tonight,' Wagner protested. 'Let Coombs and Albanese take this one.'

'Sorry, detectives, Siley's already said it's yours.'

'I bet he has,' grumbled Wagner.

Mangan laughed. 'Sarge, will you take the detectives back to the station?'

'Sure thing, captain,' said Krajcek. 'See you tomorrow.'

As Mangan walked off along the street, Wagner sucked on his cigarette. The scent of the smoke caught on Kahn's throat, and he fought the urge to light up. Something was bothering him, and he couldn't put his finger on it.

21

Albanese pointed his finger at Coombs. 'It's almost eight. You should go home.'

'Okay, Dad.'

'See you tomorrow.'

He walked down the aisle whistling a tune and headed for the back door.

She really should go home – an evening on the couch was just what she needed. Plus, her Spanish wasn't going to get any better unless she knuckled down. A shame Sal had to back out the previous night, but her cat Poirot had enjoyed most of the food she'd bought on the way back from Cresner's party.

Coombs put a Post-It note about a stolen

credit card in Wallace's cubicle. Her eyes caught another file there – it was the full ballistics report from the Pearl shooting.

Philippa Wallace must have been sleeping with someone in the department to get the results so quickly. Even in her days with the Feds, Coombs hadn't known ballistics work that fast, unless it was a serial case.

Since the move to Homicide, she'd barely spent any time with Sal. Emilio was a very good cop, and after the first few failed attempts at hitting on her, their partnership was a promising one. Siley had been threatening rotations for a few months now, and she wondered how she'd get on with Sal working side-by-side for full shifts. Maybe too well. Hell, as long as she didn't get teamed up with Harlen Wagner, things would be okay.

Coombs sat in Wallace's chair and flipped open the ballistics report. Makarov, huh? A lot of firearms were coming over these days from the former Eastern Bloc. The gun hadn't been found at the scene, but was catalogued under serial number TE9023. That meant the weapon had either been recovered since, or previously identified.

Hadn't she heard Phil saying that it was the same gun as the Simons suicide?

Coombs moved back to her computer and tapped in the serial number. A string of records came up, with links to other weapons with similar serials. Nothing strange there – if a shipment of guns hit the streets, it was likely a single gang was buying them up. She hit the record for TE9023, and the record loaded.

A shiver went down her spine – the same one she'd felt when Cresner stumbled over FID's questions. All the records were previous, going back three months. That meant the gun had come into ballistics and somehow got back out into circulation. And that meant only one thing – bent cops.

Coombs punched the number to Evidence – they'd be able to tell her if any firearms scheduled for destruction had gone missing. After the first ring, she hung up. *Slow down, Joanne.* She didn't know who was involved.

She scrolled through the records of the Pearl murder weapon. Two killings over the past six months, both members of Los Lagartos, a gang running out near Fairfax. Also some bullets pulled from the wall of a corner store after a shoot-out. The gun had been picked up on the scene of a gang murder in Wilshire, found in the hand of a dead banger called Raphael Tijando.

But from there, it somehow hit the streets again, because four weeks ago, a bullet from the same Makarov was taken from the brain of another gang member called Arsenio Ignatiez.

Now that wasn't right.

Coombs clicked through to link to the Ignatiez file. A warning popped up: *File sealed by FID, D.W.*

What the hell?

Coombs looked up and checked the Pit again, even though she knew it was empty. A catalogued weapon had reached the streets again, and been used in another murder. Wallace wouldn't thank her for butting into their homicide, but hell, she had just cleared two straightforward cases, and needed something to get her teeth into.

She stood up and walked down to the administration office, where Val Lewdizc was reading a copy of the *Enquirer*.

Coombs got as far as the filing cabinets before Lewdizc put down her magazine. 'Can I help you, detective?' she asked, staring over the rims of her half-moon spectacles.

Coombs pointed at the drawers that housed the hardcopy homicide files.

'I wanted to look up an old murder file.'

'Did you now, missy?' said Lewdizc.

Coombs felt about seven years old in the kindergarten class. 'Yes, please,' she said.

'Well, make sure you leave a note saying that you took it away,' said Lewdizc. 'I've lost count the number of times Donald Kahn or that partner of his have messed up my files.'

'Yes, ma'am,' said Coombs. She quickly found the 'I' section. It was a thin file, but the one corresponding to Ignatiez wasn't there.

'Say Val, the file I want isn't here.'

'No shit,' said the administrator. 'Is there a note?'

Coombs checked again. 'Nothing.'

'Well, in that case, it ain't a murder and I can't help you.'

Perhaps Wallace or Sal had already taken it. Or FID. She didn't want to get them into any trouble with Val, or bring any FID heat on to herself, so she sloped back to the Pit.

At her desk, Coombs checked the other Makarov incidents in COMPSTAT. A list of twenty-three incidents involving that make came up in LA. Almost all the entries fell within the last six months. Eleven fatalities. Nine of those had been gang members. Three Makarovs were taken from members of the Cuban gang, two from Los Diablos, and four from El Cuervos. The serial numbers weren't sequential but they were too damned close to be a coincidence.

The guns used in the two fatalities not involving Latino gang members, based on their serial numbers, also came from the same batch, but the victims proved to be more interesting.

Victim: Alex Demidov. Member of the Russian gang Medved. Found floating in the ocean about six months ago. Shot twice. One in the face. One in the chest.

Victim: Langdon Fisher. Found dead at the

construction site of The Immelman, a nightclub in East LA, over four months ago. Single shot to the head. Ruled a suicide. Serial number TE9021.

Again, the same batch.

Then Coombs opened up the next file. It was dated nearly seven months ago. Police raid on the Medved gang. There was a list of the gang members arrested, the list of the few that got away and ... there was Alex Demidov. There was also a list of items seized. Drugs. Cars. Pretty typical and mostly not noteworthy except for item nineteen. One hundred and twenty Makarov IJ70-17AS pistols, caliber 9 x18 (.380ACP); adjustable rear sight.

The last Makarov file was an order for destruction of the one hundred and twenty Makarovs. Destruct Team: Sergeant Brooks. Sgt. McCauley. Officers Forston and Townsend.

She added the names to her tablet.

Again, the voice in her head told her to back up. The shadow of something real nasty was looming.

Coombs headed for the break room as much to pace a little as for the coffee. There was no one in sight and the only sound she could hear was a vacuum running in some distant part of the station. And yet, she couldn't shake the feeling she was being watched. A light was on in Brooks' room and another in the temporary office that had been set up for the FID squad.

She strolled down the main hall. When she passed the slightly open door, she peered in.

No one home.

Following another glance up and down the hallway, Coombs slipped into the office. She made a mental note to leave everything as the FID staff had left it. Coombs leaned over the desk. Lots of files. Personnel files. Case files. Felon files. She gingerly lifted a couple with her index finger, then her eye caught something. The Ignatiez file sat open on the desk.

She leant over, and turned the pages under the light. On top were the crime scene photos, showing Ignatiez lying awkwardly against a low wall. Following were close-ups of the head wound and shell casing. Coombs turned the pages, which then summarized Ignatiez's record. Arrests for possession and assault going back three years. One name stood out on the reports. Arresting officer for possession – Det. Jerry Cresner.

A noise in the hall made Coombs' heart thump.

Let that be the cleaners.

She let the page fall closed, and darted to the door. Brooks got there at the same time.

'Christ!' Coombs yelled. 'You scared the shit out of me.'

'What in the hell were you doing in here?'

He looked past her into the office. 'Curiosity killed the cat, you know?'

Coombs came out into the hall and pulled the door back into the same position she found it. 'Were you sneaking around here earlier?'

'You didn't answer my question. Why were you in there? You keep nosing around and you're going to find yourself in trouble.'

She hesitated as she felt a small blush color her cheeks. 'I was just looking for a file.'

'Oh, yeah? Which one?'

'A guy called Arsenio Ignatiez.'

It was Ray's turn to go red. Coombs could tell right away the name meant something to her sergeant.

'What about him?'

'It says Jerry Cresner arrested Ignatiez for dealing a couple of years back.'

'Is that all?'

'That's all I saw, sergeant.'

The radio crackled on Brooks' chest. He was the only one in the squad who insisted on still wearing his uniform.

'All units in the vicinity, we have a hostage situation on Pandora Avenue. Suspect is armed. Repeat, Pandora Avenue...'

Brooks clicked the radio off. 'That's Jerry's road. Come on, we've got to go.'

His hand was on the small of her back guiding her toward the rear exit.

'Sergeant,' she said. 'My shift's done. I was

going to head...'

Brooks' stare became hard, angry. 'They've got it all wrong.'

Ray was acting very strange for a guy she always considered to be slow and steady. 'You know what, sergeant, I've got other things I need to check out.'

Brooks blocked her way as she tried to move past him.

'You need to learn to stand by your fellow officers, detective. Since you're poking around, asking questions, maybe I can provide you with a few answers. I'll drive.'

Coombs went with him to the parking lot. Her sense of fear was nothing but a glimmer. Ray Brooks was no danger to anyone, surely. Like Sal had said, he couldn't scare a five-year-old.

The dispatcher reported shots fired on Pandora Avenue. FID on the scene. SWAT units being dispatched.

'Get in.' Brooks ran his hand through his thinning hair. 'Damn them, if they hurt Jerry.'

As Coombs buckled her belt, Brooks turned the keys and gunned the engine.

'I don't have my vest, helmet – any of my gear,' said Coombs. 'It's in my car.'

'You're not going to need it.' Brooks flipped on the lights and siren and stepped hard on the gas.

22

'Brooks is in a hurry,' said Reyes, as they parked up at Wilcox Avenue.

'When I'm nearing my thirty, I won't be sticking around after hours, either,' said Wallace.

At her desk, Wallace picked up an open folder – the ballistics report confirmed what she already knew.

Wallace turned her attention to her phone messages – Davey was already in IR one, his wife in reception. Apparently David had called for her twice.

She put the note aside. She wondered what David wanted but didn't feel like talking with him right now. She picked up a Post-It note.

Clement Rosen. Credit Card reported stolen. Case ID SDO9-1861265-2465 San Diego.

'Hey, Sal.' Her voice sounded as tired as she felt. 'I have to check in with the Desk Sergeant. Apparently Davey's wife is out there. Davey's in the IR.'

'I'll get our shit together,' Reyes said. 'Let me know when you're ready.'

Wallace walked past the empty offices. No Siley. No FID. She pushed open the door that led to the lobby and glanced up at the clock. Just after eight. Wallace gave the civilians a onceover. A sad-looking older black couple huddled together. Ten bucks said their kid has been picked up for something and they have no idea what to do. A young Latino woman. Attractive. Coming down to pay the bail on her punk-ass boyfriend. And white woman with pursed lips and a thousand-yard stare.

Janet Davey.

Wallace stopped to talk with Sergeant Vandergriff but kept one eye on Mrs Davey. 'Did she say anything?'

Vandergriff leaned forward. 'She was noisy when she arrived, demanding, threatening, running around like a chicken with its head cut off. Since then, she's been sitting with her legs crossed, and pretty much the pissed-off expression you see now.'

'Think I need to talk to her?'

'Can't hurt, I suppose.'

Wallace crossed the room and stood in front of Davey's wife. 'Hello, Janet. Do you remember me? I'm Detective Wallace.'

She looked up. 'Yes. I remember.' She put a piece of gum into her mouth and slowly began chewing.

'Is there anything I can do for you?'

She kept chomping on her gum.

'You can tell me why you have my husband locked up in there.'

'We've arrested your husband because we think he's involved in the murder of Bartholomew Pearl and Theodore Simons.'

'That's crazy. Sam's not a killer.'

'He needs to convince us of that, Mrs Davey. There's nothing you can do for him here. I suggest you go home.'

'I bet your husband left you a long time ago, didn't he, Detective Wallace?'

The words took the wind out of Wallace's sails, and she turned and headed back toward the Pit.

'I'm back, Sal. Come on.'

He scooped up the files and followed her.

She opened the door to the interview room and held it for Reyes.

'Hello again.' Reyes placed the folders on the table, then took the end seat. He straightened the stack of manila folders and put one hand on top of them. He rested his other arm on his lap.

Wallace sat across from Davey. His face was tired, but his eyes were hard.

'Okay, Sam,' she said. 'We need to clarify a few things from our conversation earlier today.'

'I've got nothing to *clarify*. I'll wait for my attorney before I say anything else.'

'That's fine. You don't have to talk, but you still have to listen.'

Davey leaned back a little from the table and folded his arms. Wallace held a hand out

227

toward Reyes. He slid a folder to her. 'Now,' she said, 'I know that you said that the bids on the studio projects were all on the up and up. So, maybe you can answer one question for me. For a construction pro like you, it probably is an easy one to answer. It deals with erections.' She opened the folder and slid one of the photos in front of Davey.

Davey clasped his hand to his mouth, his eyes shifted from the photograph to Wallace. 'Where...' His head dropped. 'Pearl.'

'I thought I heard you say something but that can't be since you're not talking.' Wallace said. She slid out a second photo beside the first. 'Here's what I think. You were impacting Pearl's business. He told you to back off. You figured it was nothing more than tough guy talk. Pearl was a bit of thug but you weren't afraid of him. Then some of these photos show up. Sent to your house maybe? I bet there was a note that said to drop out of the bid process or the photos would be released to the public.'

Wallace tilted her head slightly. 'How am I doing?' Davey sat immobile, his gaze frozen on the photo. Wallace put another photo down. Then another.

'You couldn't allow that to happen. Your company needed the work. Oh, I know you said there was plenty of work for everyone and Sphinx Construction was as busy as ever, but, that wasn't quite true. Your income had slipped a lot in the last five years. But as desperate as you were, you couldn't risk Pearl revealing these to anyone.' Wallace dropped another picture on to the pile. 'My partner and I figured that you followed Pearl until you cornered him in the Pine Tree Motel and killed him.'

Davey took a deep breath. 'You and your partner figured wrong.' It was still a denial but now it didn't sound so self-righteous.

'Unfortunately, despite your Herculean efforts,' said Reyes, 'you couldn't find the photos.'

'I never looked.'

'Yes, you did,' Wallace said. 'Oh, how you tried. But you couldn't figure out where Pearl had hidden them. Then you got a brilliant idea. Figuring he had a partner in the blackmail – Simons, was it? – you'd send a message. You dumped Pearl's body in the Green Cheese building and torched the place.'

Davey shook his head. 'You've got it wrong, detective. I haven't seen Pearl for months. Please, take these away.'

Wallace threw the final photo on the stack. 'The blackmailer was dead but you were still worried about the pictures. You went to Pearl's apartment and started ripping the place apart, but the more you looked, the more frustrated you became. You slashed and tore and broke things and never did find the photographs. I'm sure that was eating

229

you up, wasn't it?'

Davey checked his watch and looked at the door. 'My attorney will be here soon. Please...' he pushed the photos together with his hands. '...hide these.'

'They were in Pearl's motel room after all, you know. Did he beg for his life on the floor of the bathroom?'

'I don't know what you're talking about.' Davey was starting to sound like a boxer who had gone too many rounds. Each revelation seemed to confuse him even more.

'We know you killed Pearl with a Makarov. I guess he knew you'd kill him anyway. Fixing up Simons was clever.'

Reyes cut in. 'At least two murders, arson, destruction of property, impeding an investigation ... we're talking serious shit here. We don't have to make all of it stick to put you away for a long time.'

'Yeah but you're not listening to me. I didn't do any of it.'

'A long time,' Wallace repeated.

'Look. You've got the pictures. You can see why I didn't volunteer that information. And yes, Pearl was blackmailing me, but I didn't kill him.'

The door burst open and a suited, sweating man came in with the Sergeant Vandergriff.

'You don't have to say anything to them,' he said. 'Officers, you know that anything my client has said thus far is inadmissible.'

'It's okay, Deiter, take a seat,' Davey said in a resigned voice. 'Detectives, this is Deiter Ellberg, my solicitor.'

Reyes pushed his seat beside Davey, and gestured to Ellberg to take it. He did so without acknowledgement. Reyes then sat beside Wallace. She rustled the photos again, but kept them hidden.

'Mr Davey was being a great help with our enquiries,' she said.

'Are you going to charge my client, detective?'

'Deiter...' Davey began.

'Let me handle this, Samuel,' he held up his hand. 'Detectives, this is the second time today you've brought my client across town on a whim. I will be advising him to sue for harassment.'

'Enough!' shouted Davey, losing his temper. 'I can handle this myself. The man in the photos is Robbie McCall. He models during the day and works the street at night. I've been seeing him on and off for a couple of years.'

The attorney looked confused.

'You're a regular?' asked Wallace.

'Yes.' Davey's voice was quiet again.

'Does your wife know about you and Mc-Call?'

His face twisted into a look of disbelief. 'It would probably kill her.'

'What's going on, Samuel?' asked Ellberg.

Davey put his head in both hands for a few seconds, then looked at Wallace. 'Can you give me a moment with my lawyer, Detective Wallace? I'll tell you everything you need to know after that.'

Wallace looked at Reyes, who nodded. 'Sure thing, Mr Davey. We'll be back in a couple of minutes. Take your time.'

They left the room, and Wallace pulled the door quietly behind them.

In the break room, Reyes poured them a coffee.

'You think he's gonna confess?' Reyes asked.

'I sure hope so. We cut him loose once. Twice is embarrassing and you can be sure as hell he will sue the department.'

'Then I guess it would be me shaving my chest for Vice.'

Wallace couldn't muster a laugh. 'Davey doesn't look like a cold-blooded killer, does he?'

'They probably said the same thing about Dahmer.'

She swallowed a mouthful, and took a black cup for Davey. Once they were ready to give it up, it didn't hurt to play nice.

Back in the IR, Deiter Ellberg was pale, and Davey looked resolute.

Wallace slid the coffee in front of him.

'Thanks,' he said.

'Do you want to take it from the day of Pearl's death?' said Wallace.

'Nope,' he said. 'I'll go back a bit further, if that's okay with you.' He paused.

'Go ahead,' said Wallace.

Davey took a deep breath. 'I trusted Robbie. That was the biggest mistake. I should have got suspicious when he suggested a different room to normal. Anyhow, two days after, I'm due to meet with a developer up on North Ridgewood and I notice an envelope in my in-tray. Addressed to me personally, private and confidential. Thank Christ Bridget didn't open it. I knew right away who it was from, even though there were no names.'

'Pearl?'

Davey nodded. 'It just said to keep well away from the North Ridgewood deal. Hell, I was struggling to put something together anyway. I had enough going on with the Green Cheese work. But then Sonny himself comes up to me, that son of a bitch. Right there outside the offices of Jimmy Moon. Tells me that he's taking over the business from Bart, and if I want my private life to stay private, then I give up the phase two bid. Well, that just about finished me off. I thought that by moving into private construction, that corrupt asshole at the council and Pearl wouldn't be able to touch me anymore.'

'You're talking about Simons?'

'Yeah, the good councilman. Hell, I almost flattened that bastard Sonny, but I knew that if I did, my marriage would be over.'

'So you killed Pearl?'

'I've told you, I had nothing to do with that. I may have threatened his asshole brother-in-law, but, didn't kill anybody.'

'So you deny breaking into his apartment, and then the motel room where he was staying?'

'I don't even know where his apartment is, detective, and I didn't know that he was out of jail.'

'Mr Davey, you can see where the evidence points.'

Davey sighed. 'I've told you everything – the truth. The only reason I've done so is to keep those photos away from my wife.'

Wallace stared into his face and he met her without flinching. She had the sinking feeling that he was telling the truth.

'Detectives,' said Ellberg. 'Do you have any concrete evidence at all that my client was involved with these murders? Or does your entire case rest on these photos?'

'We have a very strong motive, Mr Ellberg,' said Wallace.

'And my client has a very strong alibi for this morning. You picked him up at, what, eight o'clock? Council member Simons died before that, from what I hear...'

Wallace tried to play it cool. These smart-ass lawyers all had connections within the DA, favors to call in. 'And how have you heard that, Dieter?'

'Let's just say I've heard, detective. Are you suggesting my client killed Theodore Simons this morning before breakfast, drove home in rush-hour traffic from City Hall to his home on South Weverly, then put on his robe and met you at the door?' He cocked his head to the side. 'Come on!'

Wallace looked at Reyes. It has taken her almost an hour and twenty to get to Davey's from Burbank, though she had to swing by Reyes' place. 'It's possible,' she said.

'It's possible,' Ellberg smiled. 'But so is winning the state lottery. I think it's time to put an end to this nonsense while the LAPD still has a shred of a reputation intact. Sam here willingly submitted to a GSR, which came back negative. You seem to be victimizing my client on the dubious ground of his concealed homosexuality, and to my mind that constitutes harassment.'

Wallace felt the anger boil up inside her. Smart-ass lawyers were bad enough at the best of times.

They were even worse when they were right.

23

Small droplets of spittle sparkled in Brooks' mustache. Over the course of the twenty-minute journey, he'd been getting increasingly agitated, and his driving more erratic. Cresner the good cop – Jerry this and Jerry that.

'Served his country as a soldier, then in law enforcement. Took a damn bullet, and this is how they repay him...'

They came to a red light, and Brooks slowed, flicked on the sirens, then accelerated across the intersection.

'There was a time,' he said, 'that cops never chose between a cop and anybody else. I'd believe my partner over my own mother, God rest her soul. Now, the first hint, the tiniest suggestion that something isn't on the up and up, and our own leaders turn the FID loose on us. Nowadays, you'd better have a high-ranking friend on the force who can pull strings for you or you'll be eaten alive. I'll be glad to be rid of it.'

Coombs had hardly spoken so far. Instinct told her to hold her peace; let him calm down a bit and get back to the steady Brooks she knew. Roaring down the '02 with sirens blaring, while the driver tilts at windmills wasn't the time to point out some of the problems with his logic.

Coombs felt her stomach churn as the car went over a bump at speed. 'The DA cooked up this mess, I can tell you. I don't know why they let Pearl out, but it's their fault he ended up dead. Now they're running scared, and have FID trying to put together a case outa nothing.'

Ahead in the road a young couple scurried quickly across.

'Sergeant, maybe you should slow down.'

The dispatcher came over the radio. 'All units vicinity, we have shots fired on Pandora and Holman.'

Brooks eased the car off the freeway without signaling.

'Is that Cresner's house?' said Coombs.

'They shoulda left him alone,' said Brooks, by way of an answer.

'Maybe we should let them do their jobs,' she urged. 'Cresner might be dangerous.'

'The only person Jerry's a danger to, is Jerry,' said Brooks.

'What do you mean?'

'Jerry's got ... problems,' said Brooks. 'Sometimes he's not himself.'

'What kind of problems?'

The tyres screeched as they rounded a corner. 'Jerry's a junkie.'

'A drug addict?' Coombs had seen enough

of them to know they came in every shape and size but Cresner, well, he seemed like a different generation.

'I knew from when he first got shot,' said Brooks, 'that something wasn't right. No way should Jerry have been in that part of town. I wanted to get him on his own, but Mary was always there when I went over.'

'So Cresner was looking for a score when he was shot?'

'That's what Pearl told me.'

Suddenly Coombs was afraid. When had Brooks spoken to Pearl? Before he killed him? She was sure she could get her hand onto the Smith and Wesson CS45 tucked into her belt quicker than Brooks could try anything.

'Sergeant Brooks,' she said, 'Ray. I'm gonna ask you to stop the car and let me out. This has gone far enough.'

'Pearl wasn't a nice person. He was a total asshole in fact. He laughed at me. He laughed at Jerry too, but during his boasting, he said one thing that explained the alley, at least in part. Jerry got heavy-handed with the dealer, said he tried to cross him. Pearl got a little fresh as well, used his fists. Well, if you know Jerry, you know he wouldn't take that. He fought back. Pearl didn't know he was a cop until after he was arrested.'

Brooks turned left on to Pandora Avenue. Several blocks ahead, red and blue lights lit the neighborhood.

'Goddamn them all if they hurt Jerry.' He pulled his car up to the back bumper of a squad car. Without another word, Brooks was out of the vehicle.

Coombs followed swiftly on his heels. She glanced to the right. A small bungalow – Cresner's she guessed – was illuminated by several squad car spotlights. In the shadows like specters, dark-clothed SWAT members lurked behind trees and hunkered down on the neighbors' lawns in full gear, helmets, Kevlar vests, AR-15s, shotguns – the works. They were all focused on the little house. David Wallace was standing beside one of the cars, holding a loudspeaker.

'You need to come out now, Jerry, while it can still all be handled without anyone getting hurt.'

'Damn FID,' Brooks said. He made for Wallace.

'Wait,' Coombs said. She grasped his sleeve, but he pulled away.

'Stay back,' shouted a man's desperate voice from the house.

'None of us wants this to escalate, Jerry,' said David Wallace. 'Come out and let's talk.'

'I can't do that.'

'Hey!' Brooks yelled over the squawk of a dozen radios and the rumble of high-powered police cruiser engines. 'Hey, Wallace.'

David Wallace turned and squinted through the bright lights and spots of darkness at the figure rushing toward him. 'Sergeant? What the hell are you doing here? This is West Hollywood jurisdiction.'

'I want to know what the hell *you* think you're doing?'

'You're out of bounds, detective,' Wallace said. He pointed at him. 'Stay out of this.'

Coombs stepped into the fray. 'Wait. Everyone. We're on the same team.'

'And who the hell are you?' Wallace asked.

'Joanne Coombs. I'm with Hollywood. Ray and I are on the same squad.'

'Uh-huh, I remember. You're both interfering with an FID investigation. The suspect has already let off a couple of rounds.'

Brooks stamped his foot. 'Damn it, Jerry,' he muttered, then addressed Wallace. 'Was anybody hurt?'

'He fired into the air,' said Wallace. 'But that's not the point...'

'Listen,' Coombs said. 'Ray thinks he can get his friend to come out of there peacefully.'

'Really? Well,' he said, looking directly into Brooks' eyes, 'the only reason we haven't moved in is because your friend's wife is inside. Cresner is armed and drunk. I don't think he's going to listen to reason. We're this close to using a flash-bang on him,' Wallace said, holding his finger and thumb a quarter-inch apart. 'That's about the only way this is going to end without...'

'You don't need to use a grenade on him,' Brooks said. 'He might be drunk but he's also heavily medicated. Let me have a try at him.'

'Listen, I know he's your buddy, but...'

'At least let him try,' Coombs said. 'I don't think you want to explain the morning headlines about your squad gunning down a drunken police officer who had recently been honored for having been wounded in the line of duty.'

Wallace sucked on his lips, then spoke into his radio. 'SWAT, hold your positions. Repeat, hold your positions until I give the word.' He looked hard at Brooks. 'You really think you can get him out without...'

'Without anything.' Brooks held out his hand for the loudspeaker.

Wallace nodded and handed it to him slowly. 'Go ahead, but if it looks like he's going to lose it, I won't hesitate.'

'Understood.'

Brooks jammed down the talk button. 'Jerry. Jerry Cresner. This is Ray Brooks. I'm coming in. Go to the front door, buddy. My colleague, Joanne Coombs, is coming with me.'

'Wait a minute,' Wallace said. 'I don't want a parade going up to the house. If he opens fire...'

'He's not going to open fire. For Christ's sake, his wife is in there, isn't she? The only thing Jerry loves more than the force is his wife.'

'If he takes you both hostage, it further complicates our situation,' Wallace said.

'I'm armed,' said Coombs, patting the small of her back where the Chief's Special was concealed.

'If Jerry Cresner takes us hostage, I'll pass on my pension. Come on,' Brooks said. He started up the sidewalk. Coombs walked slightly behind and to the right. Stepping into the spotlights, knowing there was enough firepower in the darkness to blow away the neighborhood, did not make her feel confident. If Cresner panicked and fired a shot, all of those cops could open up and she and Brooks would be in no man's land.

'Jerry,' Brooks shouted. 'You had better be by that front door. I'm going to look stupid standing there ringing the bell.' Brooks and Coombs climbed the three steps to the stoop but the door didn't open. 'Jerry? Jerry, open the door. It's me, Ray.'

A slurred response, barely audible, came from inside. 'Go 'way.'

'Jerry? You let me in there, right now. You're making me look like an idiot.'

The door opened an inch. The latch was still fastened. One bleary bloodshot eye peered out. 'Ray? They think I killed that bastard.'

'Let us in, Jerry. We'll talk inside.'

The door closed. Coombs could hear the latch being moved, fumbled with. She held her breath, hoping that Cresner wouldn't pass out or do anything else to screw things up.

The door opened, slowly. First an inch, then four or five until Cresner's face was fully visible. 'You're not lying to me, are ya? You're still my friend?'

'I came here because I'm your friend.'

Cresner pulled the door open. Brooks stepped inside as soon as there was enough room to squeeze through. Coombs hesitated but only for a second. Something was telling her this was not been the smartest thing she had ever done.

'Hello,' she said, as she slipped in. 'I'm Joanne Coombs.'

Cresner nodded, and her eyes were drawn to the service issue 9mm. The barrel was pointed to the floor. 'Get in.' He quickly closed the door, and paced across the living-room. 'Ray, what the hell am I gonna do?'

'They only want to talk to you again,' Brooks said. He glanced around the room. 'Where's Mary?'

Cresner leaned against the door. It looked to Coombs like he was trying to remember where his wife was, or worse, trying to forget.

'Is she all right?' said Coombs.

'Scared to death,' Cresner said. 'I sent her away.'

'You sent her away?' Coombs asked. 'Where? When?'

'Not tellin',' he said. 'She didn't want to go. You know Mary, Ray. She didn't want to go.'

'You knew they were coming, didn't you?' Brooks said, nodding toward the front of the house.

Cresner grinned. 'I still have friends. You're my friend, aren't you Ray?'

'Yeah, Jerry, I'm your friend. Hey, isn't that the TV you got yesterday?'

The plasma was unpacked, but not yet plugged in.

'Ya. It's a damn nice one, too. HD.'

'See? That was from your friends on the force. You have lots of friends.'

'I guess ... but those guys outside...'

'It's okay. Everyone's confused, Jerry. We're going to take care of things.' Brooks nodded to Coombs. 'Could you see if you can find some coffee and make a strong pot?'

'I don't want coffee,' said Cresner. 'Let's have a drink.'

'First, let me have your gun before someone gets hurt,' said Brooks.

As soon as he said the word 'gun' Cresner's hand shot up and pointed the barrel straight at Brooks. 'Don't!' Coombs yelled, reaching for her own weapon. 'Jerry, put the gun down.'

He swivelled the gun onto her. 'Who the

244

fuck are you?'

'Steady, Jerry,' said Brooks. 'This is Joanne, remember. She's new in Homicide. Good cop, y'know.'

Coombs tensed. Cresner's hand was shaking like he was experiencing a private earthquake from a couple of feet away. There was no way she could pull her weapon.

'Jerry,' said Brooks. 'This isn't you, friend. Look at her – she's scared. She came in here to help you. She's our friend, Jerry.'

Tears pooled in the rims of Cresner's eyes then rolled down his cheeks. He whipped the gun around and put the barrel against the side of his head. 'I can't go to jail. I can't.'

'Nobody said anything about jail,' said Brooks. 'Let's put the gun down before one of us gets hurt.'

Cresner closed his eyes for a second, and Coombs leapt forward. One hand went on his wrist, the other twisted the barrel of the gun away from Cresner's head. There was no resistance, and the gun slipped into her hand. She popped the magazine.

Cresner slid down the wall until he was in a sitting position. Sobs wracked his weakened body. 'I ... I can't go to jail.'

'I'm going to tell Wallace the scene is secured,' Coombs said.

Cresner's head jerked up. His bloodshot eyes looked at Coombs, then pleadingly he turned toward Brooks. 'Don't let them come get me. You promised.'

'I'm not going to invite them in,' Coombs said. 'But if we tell them everything is okay, they will be willing to sit back and put their guns on safety. That kind of thing, you know?'

'That's all she's doing,' Brooks said.

Coombs opened the door a crack. She couldn't see anyone through the glare of the spotlights.

'Wallace? Wallace, can you hear me?'

'I hear you,' Wallace's electronically-enhanced voice boomed.

'Cresner's disarmed. His wife isn't here. Give us a few minutes.'

There was silence from the street. Coombs squinted. 'Wallace?'

'Yeah. Okay.'

Coombs went back inside. Brooks and Cresner sat together on the couch.

'Jerry,' said Brooks. 'We need to resolve the issue with the man outside. It's David Wallace from FID. You've already talked to him once before.'

'He's going to send in some of the boys and have them cuff me. I can't let them do that.'

'How about if we can get him to talk with you here in your house? Are you willing to do that?'

Cresner hesitated. 'You think he'll do that? He won't want to drag me out in cuffs?'

'I'll get him to agree to it before we take another step. Okay?'

Cresner nodded.

Brooks rose and walked to the door. He opened it but stood back. 'Wallace, I'm coming out. Everybody keep calm.'

'Go ahead,' Wallace said.

Brooks stepped outside.

'Would you mind getting me some water?' Cresner asked Coombs. 'I'm still a little unsteady on the old legs.'

Coombs didn't want to leave his side, but he stayed put as she walked toward the open-plan kitchen, found a glass on the drainer and poured water from the purifier. She set it down on the table.

'Thanks,' he said. 'Between the pain pills and the whiskey, I was pretty messed up.'

'I'd say that was an accurate description.'

He nodded. 'Damn, I'm shaking like a leaf.'

Coombs and Cresner turned toward the door as it swung open. 'We're coming in,' Brooks said.

'Okay.' Cresner slid his hands between his legs and the sofa cushion. He looked at Coombs. 'Helps relieve the pain in the hip.'

She nodded.

David Wallace kept Brooks between himself and Cresner as they eased into the room.

'Jerry, Agent Wallace has agreed to talk to you here. I told him you would answer all of his questions. Is that good for you?'

Cresner nodded. 'Yeah. Sure.'

Brooks joined Cresner on the couch. Wallace sat in a black leather recliner at an angle from him. 'Detective Cresner, I'm going to give you the opportunity to clear up a few things.'

'All right.'

'In your previous statement regarding the day you were shot, you claimed you had come upon a mugging, moved to intervene and were shot in the attempt.'

'Yes, that's what happened.'

'There's nothing you want to change?'

Cresner sat silently. Brooks leaned forward, turning slightly to be able to look into his friend's eyes. 'Jerry. Agent Wallace is giving you a chance but you've got to tell him the truth. Is there anything in your statement that you want to change?'

'Okay,' Cresner said. 'Yes. I need to change what I said.'

Wallace looked across the table. 'Please tell us why you went to meet Pearl that day.'

'I didn't go to meet with Pearl. I went to see Bunny.'

'Who's Bunny, Detective Cresner?'

'He's a ... he's my, y'know ... my dealer.'

'Bunny was supplying narcotics to you, Jerry?'

Cresner nodded. 'I injured my back a few years ago when tackling a suspect. It wasn't getting better and I was afraid that the department would force me to retire. If I visited a doctor, it could be noticed. It might be reported. I needed something to help kill the pain and let me do my job. I knew a pusher.'

'And you became a user?' Wallace asked. 'A regular?'

'Aren't you listening? I bought some stuff to help with the pain. It worked too well. It helped with all my pain. Physical. Mental. Nothing hurt anymore.'

'What happened in the alley that day?'

'When I showed up, Bunny was arguing with Pearl, but I didn't know who he was then. I waited a minute and out of the blue, Pearl started knocking Bunny around. I considered getting the hell out of there but my back was killing me and I was out of drugs. I ran down there to put a stop to it, figuring the mugger would take off.'

'Go on,' Wallace said. His tone seemed to have softened a bit.

'As I got to them, Pearl pressed a gun against Bunny's cheek. I pulled my weapon.' Cresner stopped and rubbed his chin. 'The next few seconds still aren't totally clear. As he started to turn toward me, I heard Bunny yell "Don't!" and then Pearl fired.'

'Anything else?'

'That's it. I blacked out. When I woke up, I was being wheeled into a hospital by paramedics.'

'Who called for the ambulance?'

'I don't know. It might have been Bunny – he wasn't a bad kid. Or maybe a passing good Samaritan. Not Pearl, for sure. Whoever did, saved my life.'

No one spoke. Cresner's mantle clock ticked off the seconds noisily. Everyone's eyes were on Wallace, who sat stone-faced, occasionally glancing at the door.

'Detective Cresner,' Wallace said. 'I think I believe you. I'm going to put you on house arrest until I can check out some things. I won't cover your drug habit for you, but the department does have a program. I highly recommend it. It can be a career-saver.'

Cresner nodded, dumbly. Coombs couldn't see there was much career left to save.

Wallace climbed somewhat stiffly to his feet and walked slowly toward the door. *His case has gone south*, thought Coombs. Just as he was about to leave, Wallace turned to them.

'Sergeant. Detective. I think you should meet me back at the station.' With that, he was gone.

Cresner was silent for a few seconds, then slowly pulled a .38 out from beneath the sofa cushions. Coombs heart raced for a moment, until he handed it to her, butt first.

'I wasn't going to let that asshole cuff me,' he said.

24

'Is everybody here that's here?' Siley asked, grumpily. Vandergriff said the captain had been in his hot-tub with Mrs Siley when the call came in. Siley stood behind his desk. David Wallace stood to his left.

'I think so,' Coombs said.

Brooks and Philippa sat in front of Siley's desk. Reyes stood by the door with Joanne. He'd been about to go home after they cut Davey loose, when she'd called him from Cresner's.

'In that case,' said the captain, 'I'll turn this meeting over to the FID with hopes that it won't go on too damn long. It's getting late.' He moved to the side and leaned against the file cabinet.

The door opened behind Reyes, and everyone in the room stood a little straighter, as ADA Barclay-Jones stepped into the room. 'People,' she nodded. The Assistant District Attorney took a position next to David Wallace, her arms folded. Even at this late hour, she looked like she could run a marathon.

David Wallace, on the other hand, looked tired. 'We'll try to keep it short, captain.' He flipped open a file in front of him. 'You may know that six months ago we retrieved a cache of black market weapons being sold to gangs in LA. Well, some of those weapons – Makarov pistols to be exact – never made it to the destruct. One hundred and forty were logged. One-twenty were destroyed.' Wallace turned a page, but Reyes could tell he wasn't reading from any script. He was just keeping his hands busy. 'Gangs will always find guns, but when they start shooting each other with guns that should be in our evidence vaults, it gets embarrassing. We followed up the leads as best we could from behind the scenes, until a cop got shot with a Makarov.'

'Jerry?' asked Brooks.

'That's right, sergeant. A long-standing member of the LAPD is shot late at night, in a gang-dominated area, and he's meeting a building contractor with a bad rep. We only found out it was a Makarov when the ballistics report came through. So we formed the conclusion...'

'Cut the crap,' said Brooks. 'You messed up.'

'Let the man finish,' said Siley.

The muscles in Wallace's jaw tightened. 'We may have made an error of judgement, sergeant, yes. May I remind you that Sergeant Cresner is still under house arrest pending our inquiries. We pressed Pearl inside to tell us where the Makarov came from, but he clammed up. He gave us the name of the witness, a pusher named Arsenio Ignatiez, aka Bunny. We tried to track him down, but when we did it was at a murder scene, so he wasn't much help. Pearl was facing ten to thirteen, so he offered us something else instead.'

Barclay-Jones finally looked up.

'Pearl's attorney said he could expose something rotten in the building industry in exchange for a lighter sentence. He fingered Simons. Said he'd been skimming off the top in exchange for throwing work Pearl's way. It wasn't the scalp we wanted, but it would shine a positive light on the man-hours we'd ascribed to the investigation.'

'So you let Pearl go,' Brooks scoffed. 'You let him go to keep your stats good.'

'We had no witness to confirm Cresner's story. Pearl cited self-defense. We were monitoring him,' said Barclay-Jones. 'Controlled parole. He had to sign in every morning at the nearest Precinct. We suspected that someone was helping Pearl and Simons put pressure on the other building contractors, lending a little muscle.'

'This cop you were looking for?' said Siley.

'We knew that we couldn't make the case against Cresner unless we flushed him out,' said David Wallace.

'There was no damn case to make,' said Philippa.

'Those guns got out somehow,' said her husband, coldly. 'Do you know who was on that destruct team, sergeant?'

It was Brooks' turn to color. 'I filed a report at the time saying the guns were missing. We all assumed it was a clerical error. I did the right thing. Passed it up the chain of command.'

David Wallace continued. 'If Jerry had told us the truth from the start about why he was in that alley, we could have ended this a lot sooner.'

'Sure,' said Wallace. 'And as soon as you guys got a sniff of drugs, he'd have been on his ass without a pension.'

David Wallace looked up at his wife. Reyes saw a mixture of emotions in his face. Pleading, anger, a little hatred perhaps. For a second, he felt some sympathy for the FID man.

'We have drug programs...' he began

'So are you any closer to finding out who this dirty cop is?' asked Brooks.

David Wallace looked to Barclay-Jones, who took over.

'In the face of the evidence, the District Attorney's office has decided to terminate the FID's investigation.'

Brooks spluttered. 'So what about the guns? You're happy to write them off?'

'Captain, I don't need to remind you that the LAPD needs no bad publicity. The investigation will remain open. Our official line is that Simons killed Pearl and then himself, on learning of Pearl's release. The city's a better place with both of these men out of the way.'

'Neither of those men were killers,' said Reyes, almost to himself.

'What's that, detective?' snapped the ADA.

Reyes tried to form his words without anger. 'Pearl and Simons were bad men, but neither deserved to be murdered. How come no one heard the shot in Simons' office? What about the Davey blackmail photos? Why would Simons go to that length looking for them if he was going to shoot himself in the head?'

'Simons was suffering from Post-Traumatic Stress,' said Barclay-Jones. 'He was emotional, unpredictable. We won't have a problem selling that to the press.'

Reyes was about to erupt, but Siley's stare silenced him.

'FID is turning the Simons files over to Homicide,' said Barclay-Jones. 'Get it written up quickly, and then move on.'

'FID is pulling out?' Brooks asked.

'We will still be a coordination point on the missing guns,' replied Wallace, 'but this case is to be considered *unconnected.*'

'Good night, people,' said Barclay-Jones. She walked briskly out of the room. David Wallace followed more slowly, and stopped for a moment beside Phil. He seemed about to say something, but she didn't even meet his eyes. Then he, too, was gone, closing the door behind him.

'You heard the boss,' Siley said. 'I want to see reports by tomorrow morning.'

Reyes and the others trooped out without a word.

'You okay, Sal?' Joanne asked him in the hall.

'This is bullshit,' he said. 'I didn't join Homicide for crap like this to be swept under the carpet.'

'You want to grab a coffee somewhere?'

She was looking at him with genuine concern, and in that second he knew where the evening would end if he took her up on the offer.

'You heard Siley. Phil and I have some writing up to do.'

Joanne's smile was unconvinced. 'Maybe some other time then.'

It was coming up to eleven when Reyes joined Wallace in the Pit. He brought her a steaming cup of coffee.

'Just me and you now, partner,' she said.

'Siley said Kahn and Wagner caught one off Sepulveda – they're running back now.'

'I'm not sure I can handle Harlen tonight,' said Wallace.

She pulled the desk calendar out of the

Simons' box-file. Wallace couldn't identify the feeling that twisted in her gut. Sure, she was angry. Her husband had wasted their time and withheld crucial information from her. But that wasn't the worst. Another bruise throbbed inside – embarrassment. How had FID got it so wrong? They looked like a bunch of incompetents.

Wallace checked the names on the calendar against the FID list. All but Duke had been identified and cleared. She sipped her coffee and looked through the other names, flipping back a few days, then ahead several pages. The life of a city council member seemed to include a lot of appointments, nearly a dozen some days. *Ms. Linda Thornton. Major Lee Snare, USAF Ret., Michael and Samantha Levine, Temple Beth El.*

The computer had reported no hits on Dwayne Duke. Wallace thought for a moment and re-entered the name D. Wayne Duke. Nothing.

Wallace looked for Muriel Parks' home number and dialed. Sure it was late, but the ADA wanted all the loose ends cleared up by morning, so she'd have to get over it. Mr Parks answered the phone and reluctantly agreed to let Wallace talk to his wife.

Thirty seconds passed. A soft female voice said, 'Hello?'

'Mrs Parks, this is Detective Wallace. I'm sorry to bother you but I am one of the detectives investigating Mr Simons'... suicide ... and I need your help.'

'I think I've given the police everything I know.'

'I'm trying to find out who a couple of people are. I found the name Dwayne on a sticky note. Do you know who that is?'

'Dwayne was Mr Simons' hair stylist. He works at Pierre's. I have his phone number at work if you need it.'

'Do you know his last name? Is it Duke perhaps?'

'No, sorry. That's not it, but I don't remember what it was. Pierre's has a website with their staff listed. You could check there.'

'And this hairdresser was due to see Mr Simons at seven in the morning?'

'Oh no,' said Muriel Parks. 'He phoned to say he could fit Mr Simons in first thing – probably nine o'clock.'

'Okay. Good. Do you know who Duke is?'

'I'm afraid I don't know. I arranged all of Theo's appointments, so I can't think where the name has come from.'

'Thank you so much,' Wallace said. 'I believe that's all I need for tonight.'

'Our office is closed tomorrow, of course. I'll be at home most of the day should you think of something else.'

'Thank you very much. Goodnight.'

'Goodnight.'

Wallace replaced the phone in its cradle. Maybe Siley was right. Sometimes digging didn't get you any deeper.

'Hey, Phil,' Kahn said. 'Hey, Sal. Still burning the midnight oil?'

She looked up. Wagner looked even worse than normal, and this time he had a bandage wrapped around his head.

'What the fuck happened to you?' said Reyes.

'The action got a little tasty,' said Wagner. 'Some college kids decided it was gay-bashing night.'

'Little did they know that this gay bashes back,' said Kahn.

'Siley told us about FID running off with their tails between their legs,' said Wagner, slouching in his seat beside Reyes and putting his feet up on the desk. 'Was Barclay-Jones really here? I don't know what it is about that girl, but she gets me hard.'

'Well,' said Reyes, throwing an envelope into Wagner's lap. 'These'll soften you up again.'

Wallace turned back to her desk and began typing up their response to the Simons' scene.

'If you'll excuse me, gentlemen, I have a long night ahead of...'

'No fucking way!' Wagner exclaimed. 'Hey, Don, check these out.'

Reyes was laughing. 'You're a sick puppy,

Harl,' said Kahn. 'I don't need to see that shit.'

'No, look who it is.'

Wallace turned around. Wagner was leafing through the Davey photos, and Kahn was looking over his back. 'Where d'you get these,' asked Kahn.

'They were part of a blackmail plot on the Pearl case,' said Reyes. 'The guy having a good time was one of our suspects.'

'Well, the guy having a bad time is even worse now,' said Harlen. 'He was shot dead this evening.'

25

Wallace stood up, and knocked her cup. Coffee sloshed on to her desk. 'Are you sure? Robbie McCall?'

'He was a John Doe, but there's no doubt it's him. No doubt,' said Kahn. 'Barrett will have him on ice at the morgue by now.'

'Someone didn't like his technique,' said Wagner. 'One in the head and dead.'

'Right temple? Up close?' Wallace asked.

'That's right,' said Kahn. 'Probable robbery – homicide. Where's Davey now?'

Wallace's stomach coiled with anxiety. 'We let him go. Oh shit. If he...'

'Why the fuck d'you let him go?' said Wagner.

'Wait, what time was McCall killed?' asked Reyes.

'It happened when we were there,' said Kahn. 'The blood was still dripping off the walls. About half past seven, a quarter to eight.'

'We cut Davey loose around nine-thirty,' Reyes said. 'He's clear.'

Wallace checked her notes, picked up the phone and started dialing Davey's house.

'What's up, Phil?' said Harlen.

'Don't you see?' she said. 'Someone's picking off witnesses. McCall must have been in on those pictures from the start. Someone set Davey up. They decided it was too risky to let McCall live. Pearl, Simons, McCall, even Ignatiez, they'll all connected.' The phone rang twice, three times, four times. 'The killer's still out there, and he's not stopping until he has eliminated all the risk.'

Come on, pick up!

'Hello,' a woman said.

'Mrs Davey?'

'Yes.'

'This is Detective Wallace. Is your husband available?'

'We don't want to talk to you. If you need anything, call our lawyer.'

'Mrs Davey, this is important. I've got to speak to your husband.'

'No. You've bothered him enough. If you don't stop calling...'

'His life may be in danger, ma'am.'

There was no response, only silence.

'Mrs Davey?'

'What do you mean, he might be in danger? Is this some kind of con, detective?'

'There's a serious situation developing, Mrs Davey. Please, we need to speak with your husband.'

'He's not here. He got a call from the water company. They said there was a problem at one of the construction sites so he went over to meet with them.'

'Do you know which site?'

'I don't ... no, he didn't say.'

'Does he have a cell phone?'

'Yes.'

'Can you give me the number, Mrs Davey?'

She wrote down the digits Janet gave her.

'If Sam calls, Mrs Davey, ask him to call me immediately.'

'Oh my God! He's in terrible trouble, isn't he?'

'He could be. Please, make sure he gets in touch.'

'I will,' she said and hung up.

Wallace immediately dialed the number for Davey's cell. She got his answer-phone.

Shit.

'Mr Davey, this is Detective Wallace. Can you call me urgently please as soon as you pick up this message.' She gave her number and hung up.

'Hey, Sal, get on to the water company. Find out if there's a leak at any of the Davey sites... Sal?'

'Phil, you gotta see this.' She looked up. Reyes was pale as a sheet, and he was holding a picture. 'I've found Duke,' he said, and handed over the frame. It was a photograph on a dark green border with a pine surround. 'It was tagged as being found in one of Simon's locked drawers, but there was a fade-mark on the wall that suggested it had hung there for a long time.'

Wallace looked closely at the black-and-white picture. *A Troop, 1st Squadron, 4th U.S. Cavalry, DOU6, Desert Storm* was emblazoned across the top of the photo. Five men in combat attire, standing in front of a tank. Listed below were their nicknames: *Knight, Earl, Prince, Duke, Count.*

A younger-looking Simons stood in the center. Wallace brought the picture right up to her face to inspect the figure on Simons' left. His face was cast in shade due to the brim of his hat. 'That must be Duke, but there's no way to ID him.'

'Let me see,' said Kahn. He peered over her shoulder. 'This Duke guy's your suspect, right?'

'Damn straight,' said Reyes. 'We think he may well be the cop at the centre of FID's

263

investigation, too.'

Kahn was already at his computer, tapping away at the keyboard. 'If this guy served with Simons, his records will be available at the War Library over in Gardena.'

'I don't think there'll be any librarians up at, oh...' Reyes looked at his watch '...just after eleven.'

'It's all on-line,' said Kahn. 'I've been a member since I demobbed in '93. What's the squadron?'

Reyes read off the details. Kahn clicked through several screens.

'Sal, call the water company,' said Wallace. 'We don't have time for this. Davey could be in real trouble.'

Kahn stopped tapping. 'You might be right.'

Wagner was looking at the screen, too. 'Mangan?'

'Who's Mangan?' asked Reyes.

'He's a captain over at Vice in Wilshire,' said Kahn.

'Mangan was with us tonight.'

'He's the one who made me dress up like a faggot,' said Wagner. 'I think he kinda enjoyed it...'

'Shut up, Harlen!' said Wallace. She went over to the screen. Five names were listed under A Troop. Private Eddie Wilson. Corporal Jimmy Baxter. Captain Theodore Simons. Master Sergeant Brian Mangan.

Private Ernesto Casañas. 'Mangan has to be Duke.'

'Am I missing something?' said Wagner. 'Everyone knows Mangan was out in the Gulf. So were two hundred other guys in the LAPD.'

'Yeah, but Mangan was there in an elite squad with Theodore "Prince" Simons, who killed himself this morning with a Makarov.'

'Oh,' said Wagner, as though a lightbulb had suddenly come on in his dumb head.

'Where was Mangan when McCall got shot?' asked Reyes.

'He was on the sting, with us – he'd gone to get coffee,' said Kahn. He shook his head. 'Oh fuck.'

'Let me guess, he was on the murder scene pretty promptly,' said Wallace.

Kahn and Wagner shared a look.

'That's right,' said Kahn. 'And the coffee was from Fratelli's.'

'What do you mean?' said Wallace.

Kahn scratched the stubble across his jaw. 'When he found us with the coffee, it was at least thirty minutes after he went to get it, and it was cold.'

'Jeez, Don,' said Wallace. 'Wanna tell us what you had for dinner too?'

'No, I mean stone cold, and stale. Hell, I knew something wasn't right.'

'Care to share it?' said Wagner.

Kahn was looking shaken. 'I often pick a

coffee up at the Fratelli's near Ange's place. She likes soya milk. The thing is, the place closes at seven. I bet it's the same for the one near the Biscayne.'

Reyes' eyes lit up as he twigged, along with Wallace. 'So Mangan bought the coffees earlier. To give himself an alibi.'

'He must have been the one who anonymously called in the murder to the hotel clerk,' said Wagner.

Wallace turned to Reyes. 'Sal, grab Siley from down the hall. I'm going to call the water company and see where Davey might be.'

She quickly brought up the number and dialed. The phone rang once, twice and then made a clicking noise. A recording began: 'Thank you for calling The Los Angeles Department of Water and Power. If you are experiencing an emergency situation, press nine. If you wish to discuss...'

Wallace jammed her finger on to the nine button. She could hear it click and then begin to ring. It rang several times until at last she heard 'LA Water and Power. Daniel James speaking. What is your emergency?'

'Dan, this is Detective Wallace of the Hollywood Precinct. I received a report that there is a water emergency on one of the Sphinx Construction sites. I need to know which site. Is there some way you can tell me that?'

'Hold on,' he said. Wallace tapped her pen as she waited.

'Detective?' the operative said.

'Yes?'

'We don't show any emergencies. There are three sites listed with Sphinx Construction as the primary contact. One has no water or sewer lines as yet. The other two are scheduled for completion in the next month or so and their lines are in place with no problems reported.'

'You're absolutely positive?' Wallace asked.

'I'm looking at the screen. Nothing's wrong. In fact, it's a quiet night in LA as far as we're concerned.'

'Thanks,' Wallace said. 'I'm going to need the addresses of the Sphinx sites.'

Siley came into the office with Reyes, and she held up her hand while she wrote down the information from the water company, then hung up.

'Christ!' said Siley. 'We just cleared Cresner of some bullshit charges and now you've decided to go after a highly decorated captain? You better have some strong evidence.'

'If we're right, Mangan may be out hunting down another victim as we speak. Davey's wife said he was called to one of his sites by the water company, but they report no problems. I have two addresses: the Davlene Office Complex, 6000 Wilshire and the RFBF Tower which is at 308 North Virgil.'

'If we're wrong on this one and on Mangan, we can all look forward to some dark days ahead,' said Siley. 'I've known Mangan for a lot of years, and I've never heard anyone call him Duke.'

'Maybe he and Simons only went with their old army handles when they needed security. I've sent a couple of squads to Davey's house, in case he comes back.'

'If Mangan's work up to now has been anything to judge by,' said Reyes, 'I don't think Davey's coming back.'

26

Reyes looked back and saw Kahn and Wagner turn east toward North Virgil, their sirens howling into the night. Reyes took out his cell phone and dialed SPHINX 1.

'You have reached the voicemail of Sam Davey. If you'd like to leave a message, press one...'

'He's still not picking up.'

'Maybe he doesn't have a signal,' said Wallace. She sped through an intersection under a green light.

'If he doesn't have a signal on Wilshire, he needs a new phone service.'

'He might not be on Wilshire.' There was a

fatalistic tone to Wallace's voice.

The unmarked unit's grill and dash lights and the scream of its siren cleared a path down the '02. They were making excellent time but no matter how fast they were traveling, it wasn't fast enough if Mangan was already there.

'Take the Glendale Boulevard exit.'

'Tell the units responding that we want a report as soon as they get there,' Wallace said. 'I want to know if anyone is there.'

Reyes reached for the radio but hesitated to place the call. 'I know everything seems to point to Mangan, but we all could be wrong.'

'The best thing we can do is get over there and take a look.'

The radio announced that units Baker four fifteen and two ninety-eight had arrived on the scene. Officer Diaz announced over the radio: 'The gate was open. We're in the grounds. There's a blue Continental out front. We ran the plate. It belongs to Samuel Davey. There's no sign of Davey or anyone else. Do you want us to wait or begin the search?'

'Start looking but keep your partner close,' said Reyes. 'The individual we want is Captain Brian Mangan. He should be considered extremely dangerous. You are authorized to respond with extreme prejudice if the situation warrants.'

'Repeat please. Did you say we are to apprehend an LAPD captain?'

'That's correct. And he may have a civilian with him. Samuel Davey is to be considered a hostage.'

'Roger.'

The dispatcher broke in. 'Attention units. Stand by for a physical description of suspect.'

Reyes turned the broadcast down but kept his hand on the dial. 'Hopefully with the uniforms on the scene, Mangan won't risk doing anything stupid.'

'If he's even there,' said Wallace. She left the '02 and bolted down Glendale Boulevard.

'Wallace?' Wagner's voice over the radio interrupted their conversation. She pushed the send button. 'Yeah. I hear you.'

'We're at the North Virgil site. It was locked up. We took bolt cutters to the chain on the gate. We're checking the building but it's as quiet as a grave here.'

'Thanks,' Wallace said. 'Davey's car is at our site.'

'We're on our way,' Wagner said.

'Roger.'

Wallace barely had released the send button and the radio crackled. 'Baker four fifteen. Shots fired. Officer down. Six-Zero-Zero-Zero Wilshire Boulevard. Davlene Office Complex construction site. Use caution when approaching.'

'Damn it!' Wallace yelled.

Reyes grabbed the radio 'Baker four fifteen. Adam six nineteen is ETA sixty seconds.'

'Roger. Shooter is in the building but exact location unknown.'

'Son of a bitch,' Reyes said. 'You do realize that Mangan can hear every fucking word we say?'

'Exactly.' Wallace drove at high speed through the gate. The car bounced hard. A cloud of white dust rose as she slammed on the brakes and slid to within a few feet of the main entrance of a half-built office complex. The car's headlights showed up the concrete shell of the building, surrounded by scaffolding and plastic sheeting. Stacks of builders' materials littered the yard, and a small crane stood inoperative to one side. Reyes made sure his vest was secure and climbed out of the car, grabbing his issue torch from the back seat.

'Over here,' said a voice. Two cops were crouched by one of the structural supports. Strachman and Philby. Philby was clutching her thigh, and had tied a bandage above the wound.

Her face was white as a sheet, but her eyes were alert.

'Don't worry,' said Reyes. 'The ambulance will be here any minute.'

Wallace came to his side, and Reyes

nodded toward the exposed concrete stairs inside the building. A slight breeze rustled the sheets of plastic that hung like grey specters.

'What have we got?'

'Captain Mangan hit her as soon as we hit the bottom of the stairs. I pulled her out as quickly as I could.'

'Good work,' said Reyes. 'Did you see anyone with Mangan?'

Strachman shook his head. 'Diaz and Herdez are inside. You think Davey might already be...'

'I hope not.'

'Let's get the heavy armor,' Wallace said. She moved quickly across to the trunk of the car and picked out the Colt CAR-15 5.56mm assault rifle. She shoved shells into her pocket. Reyes took a shotgun.

'Sal.'

'What?'

'Be careful.'

'No sweat.'

Wallace pulled the trunk lid down and walked back to the unfinished entryway.

'Strachman, get Philby away from the building and wait for the medics. Keep pressure on that wound. You're not safe here.'

'Aren't you gonna wait for back-up?'

'There's no time. If Mangan is in there with Davey, he's got one thing on his mind.'

Reyes opened up the channels and pushed

his radio.

'Captain Mangan. This is Detective Reyes. You have a chance to make this end peacefully. Send Mr Davey out.' Silence. 'Brian,' he said. 'We know you're up there. You know how this ends.'

Again, there was nothing.

'We do it the hard way,' said Reyes.

Wallace led the way into the building. As they entered the first floor, the wail of approaching sirens sounded out on the street, and the red and blue lights from an ambulance wheeled across the empty space. Some stud walls were half-erected – probably ready to form the lobby when the build was completed – but otherwise the building was still a shell. The walls were covered with brown paper, torn in places. Overhead the grid was installed for the ceiling tiles or lighting system but the entire HVAC conduit and piping system was still visible. A yellow rope was draped across an open elevator shaft declaring *Not in Service* for anyone dumb enough to make the mistake. Reyes twitched with each movement of the sheets of Visqueen, his heart thumping under his vest.

Wallace held up her hand, then pointed up the stairs. Reyes directed his torch. There were spots of blood, leading up the stairs to the second storey.

I hope they're Philby's, thought Reyes.

They moved swiftly but cautiously up the

staircase. Tiny pieces of construction debris crunched under Reyes' feet, and he kept his gun extended over the top of his torch. A little light penetrated from the night sky, but everything was thrown in shadow.

'Herdez?' he whispered. 'Diaz?'

Reyes shone his torch in wide arcs around the cavernous space. There were no stud walls at all yet on this floor. It was clear.

Wallace moved a little faster on the next level, and Reyes wanted her to slow down. If Mangan was waiting for them, they were in trouble. Reyes raced after her. He could feel sweat trickle down the small of his back. They move past the fourth floor and reached the landing half way to the fifth floor when Wallace pulled up short. A shuffling sound came from above. Wallace and Reyes raised their guns. A hand appeared holding an LAPD badge.

'Put down the artillery,' said Herdez. 'It's us.'

He and Diaz came into view, both holding their arms above their heads.

Wallace and Reyes rushed up the remaining steps. 'Okay, guys, what's the situation?' Reyes asked.

'The captain's taken his hostage up to the roof,' said Diaz. 'Two floors up.'

'Did you get a visual?'

'Negative, but we heard voices. The door to the outside is locked. How do you want to handle this?'

'Is there another way up?' Reyes asked.

'Yes.' Diaz stepped out of Reyes' line of sight and pointed toward the far end of the fifth floor. 'There's an emergency stairwell on the other end.'

'Take my cell,' said Wallace, handing it to Herdez. 'Call in an air support unit.'

'Sure thing, detective,' said Herdez.

'Diaz, come with us,' said Wallace.

They hurried across the empty floor toward the stairwell, with Herdez calling the Precinct about the chopper. They reached the edge of the flooring, and stepped out on to a wooden scaffold platform. The wind was strong up here, and Reyes caught his breath as he realised how exposed they were. Wallace tried a hand on the iron stair-rail, and it held firm. 'Let's hope Davey's a good builder,' she said, grimly.

Despite their best efforts, every step they took up the metal stairwell seemed to send an echoing clang into the night. Reyes switched off his torch – the ambient light was sufficient to see by, now they were out in the open.

They reached the top of the stairs, which opened straight through a gap on to the roof. No doubt this walkway would be covered at a later date, but at the moment it was open to the elements. Reyes peered over the edge. The roof was half covered with asphalt, and the other half had plastic tacked down over the tiles. Two gigantic air vents protruded in the middle, and between them stood Captain Brian Mangan. He was holding Davey close in front of him, but in a split-second he twisted and jerked up a gun.

Sparks flew from the railings over Reyes' head before he heard the crack of the shot. He almost fell back down the steps, but Wallace caught him.

'Are you hit?' asked Wallace. Reyes' heart hammered. 'Are you shot, Sal?'

Reyes righted himself on the stairs. 'I'm good. *Madre de Dios*, he's fast!'

'Get out of here,' Mangan shouted. 'You know I'll kill this son of a bitch.'

'Relax, captain,' called out Wallace. 'We just want to talk with you.'

'Don't feed me that crap, officer,' Mangan yelled back. 'I've been LAPD for fifteen years. I know what you're here to do.'

'Let's wait for air support,' said Diaz.

Reyes shook his head. 'Mangan won't let it end like that. We need to neutralize him before he sees the writing on the wall. Phil, can you cover me?'

'That depends on what you're planning to do.'

'I'm going on to the roof a different way.'

'There isn't any other way, Sal. The main stairway is locked, isn't that what you said, Diaz?'

'That's right.'

Reyes slapped the scaffolding pole at his side. 'I'm not going to use the stairs, Phil. Keep him talking, can you?'

Wallace looked at him and shook her head. 'You must be fucking kidding me, Sal...'

27

Reyes was already running down the stairs to the sixth floor. Back on the concrete he sprinted across the deserted floor and made his way across the breadth of the building. Herdez was coming off the phone by the central stairs.

'I heard a shot,' he said. 'Air support will be here in five.'

'No casualties,' said Reyes. 'You need to wait by the main stairs in case Mangan tries to come down that way.' He handed the shotgun to Herdez. 'Take this.'

Herdez nodded. 'Where are you going?'

Reyes looked skyward. 'Up on to the roof.' Herdez frowned. 'Don't ask,' Reyes added.

He continued past the lift shaft to the edge of the floor, where the plastic sheeting was tacked firmly in place to wooden jousts fixed to the concrete. There was a nail on the floor, and he used it to tear open the bottom of the sheeting and peel it back. There was no breeze at all on this side of the building – it was blowing down from the hills in the west. Downwind. Perfect. Reyes looked down over the streaming lights of Wilshire.

For a few weeks in a summer vacation while at UCLA, Reyes had worked on a construction sight, and had gotten used to carrying loads around on scaffolding. There had been guys then who used to climb up the poles like monkeys, daring each other to hang from taller heights than this, just for a couple of beers after the shift ended. Reyes had declined the dares then – he wasn't a big beer drinker and he had a healthy appreciation of danger.

As he placed his hand up and took hold of the cold metal scaffolding pole above his head, Reyes wished he'd had some practice.

Wrapping his other hand around the vertical pole, he heaved himself up, and his feet left the wooden platform. He used them to grip the pole and shimmy upward. The city spun below him, but the structure didn't budge an inch. He looked down, and his hands tightened on the pole. His mouth was dry.

Keep moving, Salvador. Keep moving.

Four feet up, and taking a deep breath, Reyes released one hand and took hold of the crosspiece. He heard Mangan's voice carry on the wind from the other side of the building.

'Don't tell me to take it easy, detective. You don't get it, do you? I got nothing to lose. Davey here's got everything to lose.'

Reyes scrambled on to the next platform, which was three feet lower than the roof-level. He caught a glimpse of Mangan, still facing toward the west side of the building, his gun aimed toward the top of the emergency stairwell. He had a three-sixty degree scan of the rooftop. Reyes lay back on the wooden scaffold platform, letting his breath still after the climb.

'You're right, captain,' shouted Wallace. 'You're holding all the cards. But no one has to get hurt here. You don't want to kill Samuel Davey. He's innocent in all this.'

'That's right, detective. You keep on talking.'

Reyes unclipped his service revolver.

What am I thinking? Mangan missed my head by a whisker at twenty-five yards.

He rolled on to his front and peered over the rim of the roof. Mangan was still standing in the open, whispering something to his hostage. Reyes was near enough to see that Davey had tears in his eyes, and was bleeding from a cut to the side of his head. His legs were almost buckled with fright, and the captain kept having to pull him up.

'Pearl and Simons were different, captain,' bellowed Wallace. 'They were crooks. I can see why you did it. But Mr Davey's different. He's a good guy. Never hurt you, never hurt anybody.'

Mangan laughed. 'Show me an honest man in the building trade, and I'll show you a broke one. They're all as bad as each other, ain't they Sam?'

Samuel Davey mumbled some words.

'Say that louder, Sam. The detective can't her ya.'

'I just want to go home,' said Davey. 'Please.'

'What's that?' howled Mangan. 'Home to your lovely wife, Sam? I had a wife once, too, God help me. Don't know what the fuck I was thinking. Come to think of it, we're not so different, though I was getting my dick sucked by a pretty *senorita* off Rosemont for free, not paying some tight-ass freshman in a rat-infested hole.'

'Please...' said Davey.

Suddenly, the thrumming of a helicopter's rotor entered Reyes' consciousness. He ducked back as Mangan arched around. The Aerospatiale B-2 Astar, nose tilted slightly forward, and angling searchlights ahead and down, ate up the air toward them.

'What do we have here?' shouted Mangan. 'You got ASD on my ass. I'm honored.'

Mangan pulled back along the roof toward the aircon housing, a curled aluminum chimney seven feet tall and five feet across, keeping Davey on a short leash.

'Please, let me go,' Davey said. 'The police already know everything.'

'Shut up,' Mangan said. 'Right now, your life has value only because those police officers over there can't shoot my ass for fear of hitting you.'

The chopper did a pass, flooding a strip of the roof with white light. Reyes saw a sniper, his feet already on the skid. Captain Mangan disappeared out of sight behind the flue.

This was Reyes' chance. He hopped into a crouch, then put both palms on the asphalt roof and vaulted over the ledge. With his gun leveled, he paced swiftly across to the HVAC unit, placing each foot with care. Mangan could pop out either side at any moment. He was ten feet away, when he saw Davey's arm sticking out the left side. Reyes went right and reached the unit. Mangan and his hostage were only six feet away on the other side.

'These dumb fucks think I won't kill you, Sam, but if you so much as fart on me, I swear I will.'

'But they'll kill you.'

'I think they'll take my pension, too,' said Mangan, laughing.

'You're crazy.'

'They call it Post-Traumatic Stress,' said Mangan. 'Driving a Humvee through a fucking minefield will do that for you.'

The helicopter came back, slower this time, and a shot erupted from the other side. It thumped into the side of the B-2, which banked away.

Shit, Brian Mangan was some shot.

Reyes checked his safety was off again, and circled the unit. Mangan was looking the other way, following the helicopter with his eyes.

'I told you I was good, didn't I, Sam?'

Reyes brought up his gun, three feet from Mangan's head, and fired.

Davey screamed, suddenly straightened and jumped off the ground. Mangan's head turned half-around, his mouth hanging open, and his eyes already dead, as blood darkened his fair hair from the exit wound beside his left temple.

His legs coiled beneath him, and Davey was almost dragged down as Mangan still gripped his collar. They seemed to struggle for a moment, with Davey scrabbling at the lifeless hand. The police captain sank to the ground. Davey pulled away, instinctively seeking shelter behind Reyes. Wallace was up on the roof in a second and running over to them, her rifle trained on Mangan. Her eyes darted back and forth between Reyes and the body.

'Is he dead?' said Davey.

Reyes lowered his gun. 'He is.'

Wallace flicked on her safety and pointed

the barrel of her rifle at the ground.

'Good work, Sal.'

Reyes stared at the expanding puddle of blood collecting under Mangan's fallen body, and beginning to trickle toward the east side of the building.

'You need to get a level up here, Mr Davey,' he said.

Samuel Davey was trembling when they got him down to the bottom of the stairs again.

'I pissed in my pants,' he whispered to Wallace.

His wife came running through the crowd and cars toward them. 'Sam! Oh, Sam. I thought... Oh my god, I'm so glad you're all right...'

She threw her arms around him, and he hugged her back, weakly.

Wallace waited until Mrs Davey released her husband.

'We need to get you checked out, Mr Davey,' she said, and led him by the elbow to the group of three ambulances that had pulled up inside the gate and where Philby was being administered to on a stretcher.

'Another one for you guys,' said Wallace. 'He took a nasty knock to the head with the butt of a firearm.'

Davey sat unsteadily on the ambulance step, then reached into his shirt pocket and pulled out a folded piece of paper.

'Detective, this is for your file.'

Wallace took the paper, and opened it up. It was a letter.

Dear Janet, I'm sorry for everything. I killed them for you. Love Sam.

'He wrote it. He was going to throw me off the roof. He killed Robbie, that bastard.'

Wallace nodded, and left Davey with his wife. She thought about their suburban house, with two cars and the range of coffee accompaniments. Sam and Janet had a lot to talk about. It would be a hard conversation, but she half-suspected they'd pull through.

The gate had been closed and several press vans had gathered outside behind a cordon. *Flies to a turd*, thought Wallace. A helicopter was circling overhead as well, no doubt from another TV crew hoping to catch a glimpse of Captain Brian Mangan, deceased.

Siley was standing to one side, with his hand on Reyes' shoulder. Wagner was smoking a cigarette beside them and offered the pack to Reyes. Sal reached out, then shook his head, as his hand flopped back to his side. He'd been high as a kite after the shooting, but now it had obviously sunk in. He looked about twenty years old. A kid. Mangan was his first.

Wallace moved closer.

'You did well,' said Wagner, exhaling a mouthful of smoke. 'Mangan was no pussycat.'

'Thanks,' said Reyes half-heartedly. 'I really didn't have any choice.'

'That's right,' said Siley. 'I've seen Mangan's type before. Cold-blooded psycho. Davey would be dead for sure, if you hadn't responded the way you did.'

The first ambulance, carrying Philby, pulled out of the lot, with paparazzi pressing their lenses up to the windows as it went. Mrs Davey accompanied her husband in the back of the second. Wallace turned to Siley.

'I guess this means the heat will be off Homicide for a bit,' she said.

Siley shrugged. 'This shit makes us all stink,' he said. 'The press will run with it for months.'

'But Cresner's name is cleared. And Ray's.'

'I guess so. Who'd want to be a cop for thirty years, huh?'

'FID should take the fall for this mess,' said Kahn, joining them. 'If they hadn't been closing our crime scenes and trying to make a case to cover their asses, we could have been on Mangan much sooner.'

'FID will slip away like nothing ever happened,' said Wagner. 'Shit don't stick to them.'

'Just shut up, will you Harlen?' snapped Wallace.

'Sorry,' said Wagner. 'We got played on this, is all.'

Wallace ignored him. 'Sal, do you want a ride home?'

'Do you mind if we stop by the Good Samaritan on the way?' he said. 'We should check on Philby.'

'Sure,' she said. The rattle of a trolley came from behind, and a stretcher loaded with a black body bag was wheeled out to the remaining ambulance.

'Taxi for Captain Mangan,' muttered Wagner to himself.

The doctors said Philby would be fine. Mangan had missed her femoral artery by a fraction of an inch, and though she'd need surgery to remove the fragments of bullet from her bone, she was expected to make a full recovery in a matter of weeks. When Wallace and Reyes left the hospital at two in the morning, she was laughing in her bed while Strachman joked about pulling the plug so he could get some compassionate leave.

They followed Herdez and Diaz to the Belgian Waffle and Pancake Palace on Franklin. The air was cool and clean, and after he'd eaten, some of the color returned to Reyes' cheeks.

'You heading home?' he asked.

Wallace thought about it. David would be up still, she knew it. He could never sleep when work was going badly. Only this time, she couldn't feel any sympathy for him. She looked at her watch. 'Our shift starts in five hours. I think I might head back to Wilcox. Finish up on the paperwork.'

'Hell, Phil, you're a machine. There's gonna be a lot of paper to shift on this one.'

'Don't I know it? You take it easy.'

'You, too. Good work, boss.'

Reyes opened the door of the waiting squad car, driven by Herdez and Diaz. 'Take me home, *amigos*.'

Wallace waved them off, then walked to her own car. In the driving seat, she placed her hands on the wheel and tried to squeeze the tears back into her eyes. A single trickle escaped. Not bad, after pulling a seventeen-hour shift.

With her right hand, she eased off her wedding ring, and held her naked hand up in front of her face. Her black skin was slightly darker where the ring had sat for ten years, but it would fade.

Maybe you're not ready for that, Philippa, she thought. *Not yet.*

She pushed the ring back on, started the ignition, and reversed out of the parking bay.